# WIPEOUT TALES

# OTHER BOOKS BY NASH BLACK

## NOVELS

*Ono County Series*
Book 1 – *Prelude of Death*
Book 2 – *Cards of Death*

*Young Brothers Series*
Book 1 – *Sandprints of Death*
Book 2 – *Catspaw of Death*

*Capital Crimes Series*
Book 1 – *Forged Blade*
Book 2 – *Honed Blade* (coming soon)

*Specter Series*
*Haints*
*Games of Death*
*Wipeout Tales*

## NON-FICTION

*Writing as a Small Business*

# NASH BLACK

# WIPEOUT TALES

## SPECTER SERIES, VOLUME THREE

Jamestown, Kentucky

*This is a work of fiction. The events and characters described in the stories are the product of the author's imagination and are not intended to refer to specific places or living persons. The author represents and warrants full ownership and/or legal right to publish all materials in this book.*

# CONTENTS

# Dedication

This volume of the Specter Series is dedicated to renowned Kentucky authors and tellers of tales Lonnie and Roberta Simpson Brown. The Browns are special friends who've been generous with their support and encouragement throughout our careers as writers.

# WIPEOUT

High pitched screech of tires burning rubber rip through the darkness. Human screams pull chunks of breath out of the night. Turbulent water rumbles and tumbles demolishing life in its path as it slices the river's banks destined for foreign shores.

The force of alien sounds pierces the stillness of time when I touch the lone trunk of an ancient tree that rises against the sky. Its jagged wind torn limbs bend over the murky waters casting twisted shadows of changing patterns. The constant movement of thick grape vines over the rising and falling of the turgid water has worn away its bark.

How is it that souls become meshed with time? Do they cling together like leeches suck poison from a diseased limb. The bogs near the river are infested with the bloodsuckers.

Stories are told of the *night washers* who inhabit river crossings, spirits who wash the clothes of the dead at night. They drag unwary travelers into the water to help them finish their chores before dawn pierces the stillness. If the

1

traveler refuses, or attempts to escape, they break his arms and leave him to drown. Evil things they are, with their hollow eyes that stare from empty sockets into one's soul and claim their victims forever.

People proclaim they don't believe the ancient stories that were told to warn their children against wandering near danger, yet no one will go near the river at night when the rushing water bulges from the gorge. They explain away the horrid sounds that shriek through the night as creaks and groans of the rust-eaten girders and beams of the old iron bridge that collapsed during the great flood and hangs in tangles from twisted piers.

I don't know what power draws me, year after year, to return and endure reliving the distant memory of terror and grief that lies buried in my soul. Is it an ancient atavistic knowledge of time long gone before civilization began? I come in the night without the freedom of choice, to make my pilgrimage to the tree. Reaching out to run my hand down it's time worn trunk, I remember when life ended and death began.

Rex, Ray, and Roy Dolen were identical triplets. No one knew who fathered them and their mother was dead. They were about twelve when the court dumped them on their grandmother, Mrs. Angus Dolen.

Mrs. Dolen lived in the little cottage across the street from my parents. In her garage was the red 1965 Pontiac

GTO convertible her husband bought, its front end twisted and torn where he'd struck a deer and was killed.

For one term, the triplets sat in my room at school, but they caught on fast, improving their reading skills so they could read the service manuals. They were driven by desire to rebuild the car their grandmother had given them.

In high school, they walked the halls like golden gods from a Viking legend. Three visions of the same person – strong and tall, blonde and blue-eyed, and a law unto themselves. They weren't arrogant as I understand the term, but simply unaware of another person outside their own existence.

Rex, Ray, and Roy never caused anyone, including their grandmother, any trouble. Their dream consumed them. They haunted Micky Stoler's garage when they weren't out rustling any kind of job to earn money to finance their car. I'd watch them from my window late at night as they counted their funds. They kept it in an old coffee tin which they buried deep in a small barrel of ten-penny nails.

On Sunday afternoons, after church, they worked on the car. I got in the habit of wandering over to watch. I'd hoist my butt up on the nail-keg and enjoy a private laugh that I was sitting on their stash. I learned new words, some my mother would have taken great exception to my using.

First, they pounded out the dents from the accident, replaced the chrome bumper and added a new radiator because the force of the crash had embedded one of the

3

telescopic supplementary headlights in the mesh. Replacing the left set of the vertical headlights cost them many trips to salvage yards and no small amount of their savings. The worst expense was getting red paint to match. That's when I learned Roy was color-blind, he couldn't tell red from green.

They weren't my friends. They may not have known my name, to them I was 'the kid'. When one yelled, "Hey Kid, get me that wrench," I preened for a week from being noticed.

I was as excited as they were the day they turned sixteen. They could get a learner's permit and enroll in Driver's Ed to obtain their driver's license. Why they named their GTO '*Wicked Kitty*' was a secret they never shared, but when one would call the car by name they'd laugh and laugh as if they'd heard a dirty joke.

The next summer brought many changes: the triplets got full-time jobs. Roy went to work for Micky Stoler at the garage, Ray found employment on nearby farms working in the tobacco fields, and Rex took a job at Merkle's Grocery in town.

~ ~ ~

Late one night, one of them pounds on our door. He's moaning and crying at the same time. His voice keeps jumping around from high to low as he stammers his grandmother is on the floor. They can't get her to speak to them. When my parents return they tell me she's dead from what appears to be a heart attack. I cry, but more for Rex, Ray, and Roy – they're alone.

After her funeral, they no longer weed her flower beds or mow the yard. Sacks of burger wrappers and pizza boxes collect by the back fence. Many, of these are torn open by opossums and raccoons searching for food. The wind catches the trash and scatters it across the yard, but the triplets ignore the mess.

The cottage is dark and dismal because they run an extension cord out a window to the garage, to have enough electricity to operate their power tools without blowing breakers. I hear them in the middle of the night easing the '*Wicked Kitty*' down the drive to take her for a test spin. A big combination lock appears on the garage doors and the windows are painted black so no one can see inside.

They spend every minute they're home souping up their car so it will go faster and faster. For a short while I continue to visit, but they never speak to me. My dad suggests I stop going over to the Dolens' as he isn't happy with the rough crowd that begins to collect while the triplets fine-tune the GTO. I couldn't see the visitors ever did anything except stand around, drink, and talk about racing. The triplets ignore them as they did me.

I turn out the lights in my room and watch from the window where no one can see me. The other guys bring beer, but I never see even one of the triplets take a drink if a bottle is shared. When things get loud my dad goes out and sits on the porch until someone sees him, then the party quiets down.

When school takes up again Rex, Ray, and Roy aren't there. They've taken the GED test and passed for an early out. When they aren't working, they polish their car. The GTO consumes every spare minute of their lives.

Everyone is talking about how they're hassling Micky Stoler to buy him out, but he's holding out for more than they can afford. They need money and want it bad enough to risk their precious car in a race. The car and the little cottage are the only things they own.

Rumors start flying about the racing, especially on Saturday night, happening on Devil's Hollow Road. It's a long road that runs through the worst farm land in the county down to an abandoned ferry on the river. It's as straight as an arrow and flat for three-eights mile until it climbs up the ridge, before it takes a sharp right turn on the crest near the barriers, to the remains of the old iron bridge. Then it runs along the cliff above the gorge for a hundred feet or so before bending to the left onto the new concrete span across the river.

The road is dark like a cave, even during the day where a canopy, made of the twisted branches of old trees bend and overlap. Rock fences line both sides of the road with white stripes running along each side showing where the pavement ends and a shallow ditch begins.

Word spreads fast when someone is looking for a race. It's a special secret that includes gambling on your favorite drivers.

Night racing in the country is always the best because you see the headlights of trouble coming for miles, especially the sheriff, who frowns on drag racing when the farmers complain the noise makes their cows go dry.

Everyone knows the Dolan brothers are working on '*Wicked Kitty*,' but no one has seen her run.

My friends bombard me with questions about how fast the dream car will go. It's fun being the center of attention of the upper classmen who want the latest scoop about the Dolen brothers' car.

I tell them little snippets about the 1965 Pontiac convertible with a 6.4 liter engine. The same one Ronnie and the Daytonas sung about in the 1960s rock song, *Little GTO*. I can't admit I've little factual knowledge of engines or their design. I repeat names of parts the triplets use basking in my newfound popularity.

They mount the engine with twin Holley four-barrel carburetors on a high rise manifold, which boosts the horsepower to a tight tension torque. Then drop a fully synchronized Stone Crusher four-speed transmission into it. They devise a rear gear ratio to give the car a high top end speed, but it dangerously limits the stability of the wheelbase. Finally they invest in and mount eight-inch wide ovals to replace the standard tires.

My bragging increases the speculation around our lockers as to how fast the Dolens' GTO really can go. Everyone is figuring ways to get out of their house without their parents knowledge on Saturday night. Many dates are made for the drive-in movie, though we all know the gate take will be low. No one intends to miss the great race, but I'm not asked to go with them. The Kid is too young to be included in their after-dark activities.

I convince my parents I've a school project that must be finished and turned in by Monday morning, when they ask me to go with them to my aunt's for an evening of playing cards. When they pull out of our driveway, I race upstairs and settle down by my window to watch and wait, the keys to my Mother's car in my hand.

It's late, almost time for my parents to return when Rex, Ray, and Roy finish their final tune-up. I watch as they high-fived each other and wipe their hands on old shop rags.

I grab my coat, stick Mother's keys in the pocket, and run downstairs to peek out the front door. They are standing in the light of the garage, their coveralls covered with grease and oil from working on the GTO. The top is down, one throws a quilt of his grandmother's over the seats and his brothers pile in without bothering to remove their dirty clothes.

I wait till they clear their drive and hotfoot it to my mother's Chrysler LeBaron. I don't have a license, but I know if I drive slowly I can get to the race.

The taillights of the GTO glow red as it heads out to Devil's Hollow Road. In the distance the sky lights up with a flash of heat lightning against the dark clouds. I reach over and turn on the radio to get some good music. The night doesn't feel right. It's thick and heavy as the wind starts picking up in sudden gusts.

On the edge of town they pull into the Parkette. I don't want to lose them, so I follow and park several spaces down where they can't see me. They order Poorboys and fries over the speaker. The voice blares from the loud speaker so I order the same with a Pepsi. I'll have little of my allowance left for the rest of the week.

Jean Folson brings out our orders. She is wearing a skirt so short her panties show. Horsing around they start giving her a big play. She gives them a high sign and skates over with my order then goes back to their car without collecting my money. She hops in the backseat and one of them joins her.

I'm shocked. They didn't ask me to go with them for all the times I fetched and carried for them. It hurts, hurts bad. I can't stop the tears that roll down my cheeks. I know then in the dimly lit parking lot I've loved them since the first day. I made a fool of myself going over and sitting on that barrel. They don't know I exist. They haven't seen that I've grown up. I'm not the Kid any longer, at least not in my heart of hearts.

I follow. I know I should go home and hide my head in shame, but no. I want to see them get beaten.

They pull into the Beverage Dock out past the city limits. Jean Folson has talked them into getting some beer to celebrate their big night. All the football team at school consider her an easy lay. It's a devastating blow to learn I'm so unimportant the guys didn't even mind talking about her in front of me. As I pass them, I stomp the gas and spin the wheels, but there isn't much you can get from an eighty-eight horsepower engine.

Cousin Brucie is spinning the great car songs from the 1960s. I turn the radio up as high as it will go to blast out the burning of my heart. The Surfaries' *Wipeout* pounds in my ears as I edge mother's car beside an old Buick in a field where the spectators' cars are parking. As the drums rise in the song's final crescendo, the sky blazes with a bolt of lightning streaking the western sky.

As I reach for the knob to turn off the radio the announcer breaks through the music to warn of a heavy rainstorm that is playing havoc with streams and rapidly moving eastward. Bursts of wind whip my skirt as I walk through the cars.

Five cars are already there, lined up on the road, their engines turning over in a low rumble of power ready to race against the clock. There is a '57 Chevy with three duces sitting on top of a high rise manifold. Another Pontiac, but it's a Tempest with a four barrel carb that has a ram air kit added, the more power boost to the engine the better. The third is a green '68 Plymouth Barracuda fastback.

Three well-built, brightly painted hot rods, cut off, and low to the back look very fast with their engines bare of a hood or fenders.

Two cars straddle the ditch with their lights pointing toward the road to where the trees tent over the asphalt. It's like looking into a dark cave, dark mouth then nothing. Several radios are turned to the same station I'd been listening to. Cousin Brucie announces he is going to play, two of the top ten hits by Jan & Dean, *Drag City* and *Dead Man's Curve*.

I remember reading about this famous duo. At the height of their popularity one of them was involved in an automobile accident. He lived to be considered a walking vegetable. I shudder. I'm scared. I'd seen the Dolens buy beer. Accidents can happen to anyone at any time. My temper fit is gone as worry replaces it: I shouldn't be here, but I don't dare go home. It's too late.

Cheers go up from the crowd as the '*Wicked Kitty*' pulls in beside one of the cut down rods. The engine roars its signal to race.

Jean Folson bounces out of the GTO with her little short skirt blowing up in the wind. She stops a man who appears to be in charge of the racing. They argue until the triplets surround her and say something to the man. I'm close enough to hear their high-pitched giggles. They're drunk!

The man hands her a white flag. She dances up to about ten feet in front of the Chevy and Tempest, prancing around in their headlights with her skirt flying.

The man uses a bullhorn to explain a change in the rules. The first two cars will peel off for a drag race to the opening into the trees. The winner will then race against one of the next two cars which will be decided by a draw from a hat. Each race will double the money in the pool. The final race is to be full out against the Dolens' GTO, from the start line to the new concrete bridge and back with the winner taking all.

I'm caught up in the crowd as they trudge down the road so they'll be at the finish line to see who wins each race. It's a relief to see openings in the stone walls that will allow the cars room to turn around on the narrow road and return to the start/finish line.

The heavy air settles around me. Even with the headlights from the cars it's dark and forbidding. All around people are drinking and laughing. It isn't a joyful sound, but nervous as if disaster lurks in the wings. Their false gaiety doesn't hide the apprehension. It's a kind of tribal expectation of a wreck as if they want to see someone wipeout. Something bad is going to happen, I can feel it.

An old man sees how short I am and lifts me up on the stone wall. From my perch I can see both ways to where the cars will come out of the trees and see the florescent painted barriers blocking the road to the old iron bridge.

The first five races move fast and smooth as silk, until the bright green hot rod is the obvious winner. Over the roar of their engines I can hear thunder building behind me, but no one else seems to be paying attention to its ominous rumble. The race they've come to see is about to begin. Big bets are being laid down among the spectators. Other people climb up on the wall, sitting with their backs to the sharp wind. It comes in penetrating gusts that cut through my coat.

We hear the roar of the start as the rain begins to fall in a hard downpour that drenches everyone. My coat is soaked as the wind whips it around my knees, a heavy wet blanket that bends my shoulders.

It's over in an instant, but my mind freezes each moment as a movie in slow motion, slowed down until individual frames are a single shot preserved forever.

The bright green hot rod and GTO shoot out of the trees neck-and-neck, their front tires covering the outside white lines. They're so close to each other only a hair's breadth separates them.

A deer jumps the far wall to land in the middle of the road facing the oncoming cars. Their bright headlights blind it and it freezes. The hot rod clips the buck sending it flying over the windshield of the GTO into the laps of Rex, Ray, and Roy.

They swerve and ride up on the open front wheel of the rod with brakes squealing. The screams of the crowd blend with the dull scraping sound of metal rubbing against rubber.

I hear my own voice yelling, "No! No!"

All heads turn to stare in terrified horror as the locked cars roar past where we're standing.

The watchers surge into the sheets of blinding rain, eager to get to the wreck. I'm bumped along in their wake, fall in the mud, get up to keep from being trampled by the panicked mob.

I scream, "The curve! The curve!" as if they can hear me through the driving rain.

An immense crash of disintegrating steel grinding against iron tears through the night. The scene lights up in a fiery blaze as lightning strikes a tree followed by a loud crack, like a gunshot of thunder. The inferno illuminates the cars locked in a deadly duel. They sail off the remains of the old bridge into space. For a brief moment they hang suspended in time.

I fight my way through the crowd to the edge of the cliff leaning over to see where the GTO lands. The edge gives way under my feet. I plunge into the darkness of the gnarled roots of a tree on the bank of the river.

The moon breaks through the tumbling clouds for a lost moment in time. The hot rod is on its side below me, the front end buried in the muddy bank of the river. Jean Folson dangles half-in and half-out of the window. She'd hitched a ride to death.

A thin shaft of light strikes the undercarriage of the GTO, nose down in the turbulent water, the big back tires still spinning. It dances and bobs in the muddy river slowly turning like a ballerina executing a perfect pirouette.

I know Rex, Ray, and Roy Dolen are dead without being told. I'm too numb to feel the grief that overwhelms me.

The *night washers* rise out of the murky water, eerie shapes of nothing pulling the clothes from the dead. A mist undulates near the trunk of the GTO. One of the evil things is tugging on Mrs. Dolen's quilt. It's streaked with stains.

I stretch and reach for it in the swirling water. I'll not let the death creatures take the quilt. Mrs. Dolen taught me how to make the tiny stitches in each block before Rex, Ray, and Roy came to live with her. She said it would be a present on my wedding day. Until then she'd keep it on her bed for me.

Suddenly, a wall of water surges from the gorge pushing a mass of broken trees and trash, twirling and spinning the hot rod away by its force.

The GTO vanishes.

I hear through the darkness of my mind, voices shouting and giving orders.

"No hope for them."

"She's alive."

"Get her out of here."

"Be careful."

A wall of pain engulfs me: grief for my lost friends, physical pain from broken bones grinding together. It is the last agony I feel for a long time.

~ ~ ~

While I'm in the hospital, Micky Stoler brings the GTO home to the garage across from my parent's home. The quilt is draped across the broken windshield.

The little cottage sits abandoned and forlorn. Weeds and trees grow in the driveway. The roof blew away in another storm. Its porch has collapsed and sags from rotting boards. A little cedar tree found root in a twisted gutter.

At night, when the light comes on in the garage, I sit on the porch and watch Rex, Ray, and Roy Dolen tune and polish the Pontiac GTO, while Cousin Brucie spins *Wipeout*.

# THE SHOP

Ted heard the ad on the radio for employment at a place called The Shop.

"No experience necessary. Apply in room 725 at *The Shop's Bar & Grill* on Phillip's Drive each morning from 5 to 7AM. Come early for a good breakfast. The grill is open 24-7."

Ted got up early the next morning to go to the grill for his breakfast and to apply for the job. When Ted's waiter brought him the check, he asked, "Have you come to apply for the job that was advertised on the radio yesterday?"

"Yes, I have."

"Follow me. There'll be no charge for the meal if you're hired."

"Are there other openings to be filled?"

"Just the one."

The waiter led Ted down a hall and through the kitchen to room 725. When they got there the waiter knocked on the door twice.

"Wait here. Don't move from this spot. They'll come for you when they're ready."

The waiter vanished before his eyes as he turned and went back down the dark hall. Ted waited for what seemed like an eternity before someone came for him.

The door slowly opened allowing a dim light to shine into the hall.

"Come in. What is your name?"

"Ted Richards."

The man pointed to a chair across the room.

"Pull up a chair. My waiter tells me you're looking for work."

"Yes, Sir."

"How did you hear about The Shop?"

"I heard a commercial on the radio that you were looking for a worker with no experience."

"Ted, you have just been hired as our new project starter. There are no forms for you to fill out. We take care of the paperwork for you. It won't be necessary for you to pay any Federal Income Tax or Social Security taxes. We take care of any financial obligation to federal, city, and state governments."

Ted was glad to hear he didn't have to bother with paperwork. He'd always preferred to be paid in cash under the table.

"This is a small specialty shop. We have one client. He lets us know what to build and how many units are required.

"Browse through this project book of what we're now building after supper tonight. We build what's in this book to our client's specifications."

Ted took the heavy volume the man handed him. If he read all the specs in this book he'd be up half the night.

"You're not allowed to build anything but what you are instructed to. This is your only warning. You will need to learn all the shops rules and regulations."

The man handed him a second blue bound volume that was almost as thick as the project book.

"The Shop will take care of all your needs until your employment terminates. You will eat, sleep and work here.

"If you have a cell phone or any other means of communication to the outside world leave it in the box on the corner of this desk. You will have no further need for them. That includes your watch."

Ted had heard of closed union shops and tight security, but this guy was dead serious. Old crank face hadn't smiled the entire time he was pitching orders.

"When you walked through the door of *The Shop's Bar & Grill* it was the last time you will see the outside world during the term of your employment."

"Your waiter is on his way up. Take your place outside the door and he will be with you shortly. Be sure to stand on the marks provided on the floor. That will be all."

Ted went out into the hall and stood where he was

instructed. A few moments later the floor felt warm through the soles of his loafers.

Balls of cloudy white light began flying up and down the hall bouncing off of the walls and ceiling. Lightning bolts danced about the floor and around his feet.

His feet got warmer, but he was unable to move them. They were stuck to the floor. The heat was melting the soles of his shoes!

Ted didn't know what was going on, but he wished the waiter would hurry. His legs were starting to ache from standing in one place for so long.

Finally, he could see the waiter coming up the pitch black hall kicking the balls of light and the lightning bolts out of the way. Every time the waiter kicked one they became brighter and rumbled, sounding like thunder. When a lightning bolt struck the wall, the wall shook.

"Come with me, Ted. I'll take you to your room. It's on the lower level below The Shop."

The waiter took his hand. The floor opened. They dropped to the lower level.

"Your room is at the end of this hall. You study in room 113. It's one of our smaller rooms. That section of rooms is reserved for the new recruits. They're below the restaurant.

"Your meals have been planned for you and will be sent down at the scheduled times. Breakfast is at 6 am. Other meals are every six hours after that.

"You have plenty of soft drinks and snacks in your room. You will need them when your studies begin. All the clothes you will need are in the closet in your bedroom. The Shop provides the basic necessities for your study and work."

Ted had never been in the army, but this guy sounded and acted like the sergeants he'd seen on TV.

"You will work in the shop twelve hours a day – five days a week. You get a ten-minute break every three hours. On weekends you will study ten hours a day except for Sunday, where you can spend time the gym or rec room on a prescheduled basis. Church services are provided in the cafeteria after breakfast.

"Your books are on the desk in the bedroom. A study schedule has already been provided. You will start one hour after I leave this room.

"You will study on the same schedule as your work schedule. Your course of studies are three months long after which time you will start to work in the shop. There are no television, radio, or clocks in the room. The bathroom is a small cubicle in one corner. You will be told what you need to know as you need to know it.

"After I leave this room, I suggest you change from your street clothes into your uniform. You'll have no further use of them. Your actions will be monitored. Obey the rules and you will not be punished. When I leave, the door will not be opened again till the end of your studies. The door will not open from the inside. That's all the instructions I have for now. I suggest you get to work."

As the door closed on the waiter, Ted felt a shudder of fear run down his spine. He began to wonder if he'd let his pressing need for a job lead him into a situation he couldn't handle. The strict regimentation was outside his experience. He'd always been a laid back guy who took life as it was handed to him and didn't ask questions.

Ted changed into his uniform and went to the desk where he found the lesson plans. There were step-by-step instructions on what to study and when to study each subject. Ted felt a distinct urge to change the instructions for the hell of it, but changed his mind.

The first chapter explained most of what his waiter had said. It suggested he spend the rest of the day reviewing book one. So deep below The Shop, without his watch, he realized he had no way of knowing night from day.

Ted knew he was being watched. The walls were covered with small round holes that kept opening and closing. He could hear faint voices and what sounded like cries coming from outside the room.

His meals came on schedule. They were passed through the wall and placed on the table across from the foot of his bed. A note on the tray said,

*You have twenty minutes to eat. The food tray will then be removed, even if you are not finished eating.*

Another note reminded him that he could find snacks in the cooler under the table. The first snack break was three hours after he'd eaten his first meal. He'd have ten minutes. The snack and the cooler could not be opened until the next snack time. Then the next meal would be three hours later. There would be nothing more to eat until breakfast at 6 am. Lights would be turned off at 9:00 pm.

The only light in the room, after lights-out, was the light on his desk. It was enough to rapidly change clothes for bed before it too went dark.

During the night he was woken by a figure standing at the foot of the bed waving a stick over him. He sat up hoping to get a better look of the foggy mass, but when he did, the specter jumped to the ceiling waving its stick over the bed.

When Ted got out of bed, the faint glow of the figure ran across the ceiling to disappear in the corner of the room. After that, he couldn't get back into sound sleep. He tossed and turned until wake-up at 5:30 am when all the lights came back on. This gave him a half hour to shower. There was no razor in the bathroom so a shave was impossible. He got into his uniform and was ready for breakfast to come through the wall. He would have enjoyed a cigarette while finishing his coffee, but his own clothes had disappeared.

Ted went to the desk to begin his studies. The books weren't stacked on the corner of the desk where he'd left them. They were under the desk on the floor. The pages of the top book on woodworking tools and machines was being turned, as if they were being read.

He yelled. The pages stopped turning. The books floated back up onto the desk to where he'd left them the night before. The chair slid under the desk where it should have been, not over near the bathroom cubical.

He studied books on woodworking tools, machines, and procedures for the next week. The only way he could tell how long he'd been studying was by the number of sleep cycles. After he finished a topic, that book was removed from the room during the night while he slept.

The next topic listed on the lesson planner was welding, brazing, flame cutting and making foundry molds. Their techniques took more concentration than he'd ever used in his life, just to understand the terminology of each operation, let alone how to perform it. Also included in flame cutting was flame welding. This was an area that he had always been interested in since he'd walked through a machine shop at a vocational school.

The books for these topics were much thicker than the ones on woodworking. But the schedule was set as to how many pages he had to cover each day. Books were okay, but he was a hands-on man and wished he had an area where he could practice.

Ted was groggy, like his brain was in a thick fog. The constant sameness of study, snack, eat, sleep became his concept of time.

Nights became a familiar repeating nightmare. Sounds he could not identify seeped through the walls. Figures came down from the ceiling to occupy his room, using their sticks to hit the walls and his bed. It seemed like a deliberate attempt to kept him awake. He dreaded lying down, as if by staying awake, he could keep his terrors at bay. As exhaustion overwhelmed him, these too merged into fragments of mists.

The nightly visits took time away from his studies, as he had to straighten his room every morning because the books had been scattered around the room during the night. He began to feel a tension close to panic, wondering if he could ever finish the studies and be assigned to work. Would he have absorbed enough information to do the job he was hired to do?

Ceramics was the last area listed in the program of studies. As a child, Ted had watched his grandmother make and use molds for Kewpie Dolls and masks, for carnivals and booths at county fairs.

She would place a pattern in the bottom half of a mold and pack sand around it. Next she would put the top half on the bottom half and pour sand over the pattern, packing it down. Then, the two halves, were held together with rubber bands, cut out of automobile tire inner tubes. She pored liquid clay into openings on top of the mold until it overflowed. She let him tilt the mold back and forth to get the air bubbles out, which was fun.

The mold was then set aside for a few days, so the clay could dry to the desired thickness of the pattern. Whatever was in the mold was then taken out and allowed to dry for several more days before she would trim the rough edges, to prepare it for the first firing in the stone oven. He helped her pump the billows to keep the fire hot. When the figures cooled she painted them wonderful colors and dipped them in a liquid glass glaze. Then she fired them a second time to set the finish.

The flash of memory penetrated the murkiness that had clouded his mind for days. He knew the ropes by heart, and besides, the procedure for making foundry molds was much the same. He could ace this section with no sweat.

Modern molds where made of a product that would withstand the high firing temperatures of the kiln. The temperatures would be a thousand times higher than his grandmother could produce with the bellows she salvaged from an old blacksmith's shop, in the stone oven that was built along the lines of a smoke house.

Making foundry molds hadn't changed for years. In modern mold making, a wax pattern was placed in the mold. The bottom half of the mold was packed with sand, a pattern was placed in the middle, the top half of the mold was then placed on top of the pattern, with more sand packed on it leaving two holes.

One hole was where the molten steel was poured in, on the pattern. When the mold filled, the excess molten steel came out of the other hole. Next the mold was left to cool before the item was taken out of the mold. The sand was then shaken off the item and the edges were trimmed. Finally, the molded items were sent to a machine shop for finishing and polishing.

His evening meal arrived with a note saying:

*You are doing a good job with your studies. There will be one last book on your tray with your breakfast. Follow the instructions carefully.*

Breakfast and the last book arrived promptly, as had all the rest. After eating Ted read the note that was attached to the wrapping that covered the book.

*This is your last book in the course of your studies. You have three months to finish it and thoroughly understand everything in it. Your future depends on it. Now unwrap the book.*

The book was a Bible.

He studied all day, stopping only for rapidly consumed meals.

The further he got into the Bible the more he became aware that the sleep disrupting actions of the figures floating around his room during the night and the sounds coming through the walls and the ceiling slowly ceased.

The feeling of being alone, truly alone, since the first day he'd entered *The Shops Bar & Grill* was great.

One morning his breakfast tray had a liberating note.

*Your three months are finished. You've done a good job. You have one hour to finish your breakfast and to get ready to join the rest of the working team. Your waiter will come for you. Please be ready. Your door won't open until he comes for you.*

~ ~ ~

"Come with me, Ted. I've been instructed to take you up to your new quarters – room 10, which is down the hall from the entrance to The Shop. Here is a procedures book. Study it until your shop foreman comes for you."

This man wasn't the same person Ted had first met as his waiter. Ted didn't say anything, but out of the corner of his eye he studied him.

The Stranger wore a white jumpsuit. He was huge, near six and a half feet or more. His shoulders were so broad they filled the doorway to the room. He walked Ted up long iron stairs built into a narrow opening between two solid walls. The new room he'd been assigned was much like the one he'd just left. He dumped his duffle on the bed and turned to another stranger, who'd followed him into the sparse room.

This man was short, rather on the stocky side, but from the way he moved Ted assumed the bulk was muscle, instead of fat.

28

He wore a red jumpsuit.

"I'm Mr. Andy, your shop foreman. If you need anything ask for me. For now, as a new man in the shop your duties will consist of keeping the machines, the floors, and the restrooms clean.

"Located against the wall, near the middle of the complex, are individual waste containers for wood, metal and ceramic scraps. The container for metal includes all the scrap from the welding shop, foundry and the machine shop. People from the outside pick up the containers once a week.

"Your cleaning tools can be found in the closet, opposite the waste containers. The metals room must be kept clean and orderly at all times. It will be inspected without notice.

"Your meals and snacks will be on the same schedule they were on during your studies. We work twelve hours a day, five days a week.

"You will be expected to study the shop procedure manual in the evening after your dinner until lights-out and in the morning before your breakfast. If you do a satisfactory job while on probation you'll be promoted to a job that we see is fit for you as an apprentice.

"Promotions are given by a board of directors who oversee the performance of all the workers. You had best get to work. It's been a while since the shop has had a thorough cleaning. You can start with the restrooms."

The words rolled off Mr. Andy's tongue in a flat, dry cadence as if he was reading a poster he'd read many times before. Ted was grateful to hear the dull tones as he realized this was the first human voice he'd heard since the waiter brought him to his first assigned room, before he began the long months of studies.

Mr. Andy turned with a military about face and beckoned Ted to follow him. They entered the machine shop. Mr. Andy pointed to the broom closet and walked away.

When Ted opened the closet door, the tools flew out followed by sharp screams of death. He tried grabbing for one of the cleaning tools, but it would take off in another direction, with screams following them. Finally, the tools fell to the floor.

They were scattered all over the shop. Some tangled in the machines, some twisted around the light fixtures. It wasn't until just before lunch that Ted got them gathered up and back in the closet. Foreman Andy wasn't wrong when he told him the shop was a mess. It was a hell-of-a-way to give a new custodian a full tour of the facilities.

Ted wondered how long it had been since The Shop had a new employee as he scrubbed and cleaned the filthy restroom. It was obvious this was where the men were allowed to shave their beards as the drains were clogged with hair. The buzzer for the end-of-the-shift sounded just as he hung the last cleaning rag on a pole in the closet. The Stranger appeared at his elbow and walked him back to his room.

Sounds of cries, as well as laughter, came out of the walls and ceilings from every department. Ted stumbled once, he was that tired after months of sitting on his fanny over a book. The Stranger caught Ted's elbow and helped him stay on his feet, then unlocked the door to room 10, the room to which Ted had been assigned.

"Use your time wisely before lights-out. You have a lot to learn if you expect to advance. I'll be back for you shortly after the wake-up buzzer sounds. You won't have much time after that for breakfast, before the work buzzer sounds. If you miss breakfast you'll get nothing to eat until snack time. You might even get punished and not be allowed to eat until the evening meal."

Ted heard the distinct heavy click of the lock in the door. He fell on the hamburger and fries like a starving man. Then he staggered to the wash cubicle for a quick shower, before he took up more bookwork.

His studying and sleeping were both disrupted, most of the night by screams and cries from the machine shop. Even in the dark he could see gray transparent outlines of people and debris, like the metal scraps he'd picked up during the afternoon were floating around his room.

When the Stranger came for him in the morning, Ted wasn't completely dressed. He managed to finish snapping the closings to the green jumpsuit by the time they reached the cafeteria. There were other men in the large room, scattered around at assigned seats too far apart for any conversation. A tray of food was at his assigned seat. After the night he'd passed, he welcomed the silence.

The metals area was Ted's next cleaning assignment. It wasn't too dirty for not being cleaned in such a long time. He was taking scraps to the trash containers when he noticed everything he'd cleaned the day before was covered with the debris he'd seen floating around his room during the night.

As he emptied his wheelbarrow into the dumpster, Ted heard, but could not see, two people talking. He knew he was being watched and didn't want to get into trouble, but he was determine to hear what was being said. He stumbled and tipped the wheelbarrow just short of the dumpster.

The voices were discussing something they called Gray People. They believed it was those so-called Gray people who came from a nearby dump, during the night where all the scrap taken. The Gray People were invisible to humans, but were everywhere, causing untold extra labor for The Shop employees.

Some went back to the dump where they lived, while others stayed in the building, waiting for everyone to leave for the day to vandalize the shop. Those that were there during the day did their best to disrupt production by disabling machines and moving scrap containers to different departments, then emptying them over the machines.

Ted knew he'd taken more time than necessary for this load and hurried back to work. Somehow he'd been able to keep up with all the disruptions created during the day. But when he took time to look at his loads, he noticed he was carting the same scrap over and over to the dumpster.

He was glad to hear the end of the day buzzer. There was a short wait for the Stranger to come to walk him back to his room. Ted spent the time thinking about what he'd learned and making some vague plans to find out what-in-the-hell was going on at The Shop.

"Come, there is a book on the table in your room. Study it tonight. The company's client has placed a large order for some ceramic pieces. They've put the rush on the order. The Ceramic Department is short-handed. You have been moved to fill the position. Try to get some sleep tonight. Don't be late in the morning."

The Stranger invited no comment. His flat dull voice belted out commands. Ted figured if he'd tried to cut-and-run, those broad flat hands would beak his neck without a second thought. He'd let himself get caught and caged like a circus lion who moved when the ringmaster cracked the whip. He intended to go on living.

That night was like many he'd experienced while he was a student, but this time he studied the thin outlines that floated above his head. When he saw the odd, crushed brass shell casings – he knew. The debris floating around his room was the same from the wheelbarrow loads he'd spent the day collecting in the metals workroom.

He wanted to scream, but at the moment his conscious mind made the connection, the noise stopped. The images disappeared and his rest was peaceful.

The Stranger unlocked his room door just as he snapped the last grip on his uniform. They walked to the cafeteria, ate the waiting meal. He escorted Ted through the building to the ceramics department, opened the door and pointed from him to enter. A young man with rusty red hair and green eyes waited by the entrance.

"You must be, Ted? I'm Frank, the ceramic department group leader. You know we have a large rush order to fill, but first, twelve new kilns came in during the night. They must be installed before we can begin the project.

"It looks like we're in luck the Gray People haven't bothered them over night."

Frank's casual use of the term, Gray People startled Ted. The voices he'd heard at the dumpster had seem furtive and hidden, like they were discussing a horrible secret. He didn't interrupt Frank to ask questions. He was afraid to learn the answers.

It hadn't taken long for Ted to figure out the colors of the jumpsuits were an indication of rank in the workforce. Frank wore a black one.

"Your job is to build shelves strong enough to hold the new equipment, next to the other kilns. An electrician will run the wiring after you get them finished."

His first real assignment flooded Ted with relief. Building shelves was kids work. Allowing time for precise measurements, cutting the planks, and constructing the brackets was an easy job.

A day and a half should do it.

"Frank, the shelves should be ready by break time in the morning."

Ted was true to his word and reported the finished shelves to Frank. He sent him, with no escort, just simple directions to the Electronics Department to obtain an electrician to finish the installation project.

There were no locked doors. The man at the desk smiled as he opened the door.

"I'm from the Ceramics Department. We have twelve new kilns that need to be wired up in the morning. Do you have an opening on your schedule?"

"Yes, I can work that in for you."

"Thank you. My name is Ted. Your name is?"

"Sam."

"Nice meeting you. See you in the morning."

"Okay, Ted, I'll bring my tools, the wire I'll need, to your department just before break-time. If I were to bring them to the job site this afternoon the Gray People will have them before morning. I must keep them locked down until I'm ready to use them."

As he walked back to the Ceramics Department, Ted pondered Sam's reference to the Gray People stealing their tools and materials. Mr. Andy in metals had never mentioned them, though it was easy to see the chaos their activities produced on the shop floor. He puzzled a moment as he entered ceramics – he'd never seen Mr. Andy around the metals department after their first meeting.

"Frank, I've contacted the electrician. He put us on his schedule for in the morning, just before break-time."

Sam the electrician and Ted hit it off right away working together. They had a chance to talk while installing the heavy electric cables.

Sam told Ted he'd wandered into the restaurant for lunch and the waiter asked him if he was looking for work.

"Yes, I could use some work. I'm between jobs at the moment."

"If you're finished eating, come with me."

Sam was instructed to wait. The time seemed like an eternity. Bloodcurdling screams came out of the walls with balls of light and lightning bolts bouncing around. A door opened. A voice from the chair behind the desk instructed him as to what was expected of him. "Do your work, stay out of trouble or else you well be punished. You will be furnished with everything you need by the Company."

"Sam, the same thing that happened to me!"

"Well, Ted, here I am. Let's get started. I'll place the electric boxes every forty inches apart on center. That will give them enough room between each one so they won't overheat when in use. I'll have to set a new breaker box for each kiln. That will put each one on its own circuit, so if one goes down you can still use the rest of them."

"Can I start putting the kilns on the shelves?"

"That'll be okay. I've tested each connection as I connected it to the main line. We'll plug them in, one at a time and turn them on to test each kiln. If the kilns are not defective everything should work. Fire them up, Ted, bring each one up to a temperature of twelve hundred degrees.

"Everything appears to be running smooth. Do you have anything ready to fire?"

"Not yet. We have two-dozen molds poured, but they won't be opened until tomorrow night. We must be very careful to follow a set procedure to prevent shrinkage and warping."

Ted was delighted to have an interested party listen to how ceramics were created. He knew part of it wasn't showing off, but a response to how lonely he'd been during the long months of study.

"The extra clay will need to be poured off. Pieces must dry in the molds for a day before they can be removed. Then, they're trimmed to make them ready for the first firing. After that, they have to be slow cooled to make them ready to paint. The paint is allowed to air dry, then an over glaze of liquid glass is applied before they are fired a second time. The finished pieces must again cool before they can be packed and shipped.

"It will take three months to complete this order."

"I don't envy you guys one bit. I'll stick to running wires."

Ted watched Sam leave. He knew he'd miss having someone to talk to. He turned out the lights as the dinner buzzer sounded.

Later, he'd seen Sam in the cafeteria, but the man walked by him without speaking as if he didn't know him.

~ ~ ~

"Ted, we now have an order for gun stocks. You've been chosen to make them. We have some blanks in the wood rack."

Ted had been happy working with the kilns and had ceased to worry about what was happening around him. Frank was an easy boss to work for and allowed Ted extra time and drinks away for the hot ovens. He didn't want to be moved to another department. He hesitated to answer but knew that to refuse a move to another department was a death knell with the Company.

"I've never tried to build gun stocks. It might be fun."

"Come on, I'll show you where the blanks are located."

They walked back to the wood room. Ted got the blanks off of the rack and took them to his shop desk. He got out the plan book and laid out the blanks according to the plans.

He took the blanks to the lathe to begin working them. While turning down the first blank it split. Pieces flew out of the lathe. A chunk hit Ted in the forehead penetrating his skull, rendering him unconscious.

Frank tried to revive Ted with simple first-aid but wasn't having much luck. An accident like this was out of his league – it was time for emergency services.

EMS arrived on the scene from the shop's infirmary. "What do we have here?"

"Ted got knocked out when a chunk of wood came flying out of the lathe. He's out cold. I swear one of those Gray People hit the machine knocking the piece of stock loose."

"Here, try smelling salts again while I set up the heart monitor. I'll get his blood pressure.

"His BP is extremely low 40/90. Try CPR."

"It's not working!"

"His heartbeat is very weak. I can hardly hear it through this stethoscope.

"We don't have a choice. Get him ready to transport while I call it in to let them know we're on our way."

The Shop's hospital was across town from the factory buildings. It was a public relations gift from the Company to smooth over local opposition to the building of The Shop.

Frank was worried. He knew Ted had set up the lathe by the book. He'd never had an accident of this magnitude happen on his shift. What if the kid died? He could lose his job.

"Bill, finish these stocks. I'm going to the hospital with Ted. If I don't get back this afternoon put the electronic handle across those saw blades on the wall in my office. Make sure all doors are locked if I'm not back by quitting time."

By the time they reached the hospital, Ted had slipped into a coma. Nurses were pushing the gurney into the emergency room before Frank and the Company doctor got through the door.

It was maddening for Frank to be shunted aside and be told to wait outside. He'd seen them start an IV and hook Ted up to a couple of machines to monitor his vital signs.

An hour later, their own doctor gave Frank the score. The news wasn't good. He knew all hell would break loose when the directors found out one of their employees was in a hospital, barely alive.

"They're going to admit him so they can do tests. He is in isolation. No visitors. There is nothing you can do, go back to work and put a lid on it."

Frank knew the least of his problems would be the mass of paperwork he'd have to fill out before he could call it a day. He'd been lucky to hitch a ride in the ambulance as The Shop was opposed to their employees leaving the grounds.

He took a taxi back to the plant and managed to sneak in beside an empty dumpster moving into the building on a track. Bill was the only person who knew he'd left the premises. He didn't think the little Oriental would squeal. The Enforcers of The Company's rules could deliver a world of hurt before they killed him.

~ ~ ~

In the distance Ted could hear two women talking, but he didn't have the strength to open his eyes. His face felt funny, it wasn't itching. He'd been shaved – it felt good though he'd grown accustom to the beard.

"It looks as if he might have massive brain injuries."

"I don't know what to say. They said they thought he had a good chance of coming out of it last night."

It took Ted over a month to fully recover from the sharp blow that had left a slow healing hole in his forehead, but no permanent damage. The doctors assured him he was very lucky to have survived.

He was transported back to The Shop in a closed van, but not before he caught a glimpse of a bank sign showing date and time. He was shocked to learn it had been eleven months since the day he'd entered the Grill and asked for a job.

He was escorted to the ceramic department when he got back, as if he'd never been away, but his place in the cafeteria had been moved to a far, dark corner.

Sam was wearing a dark blue jumpsuit. He had gotten a promotion since Ted had last seen him. He wandered past Ted as he was lifting raw molds into a kiln for their first firing on the pretense of inspecting the wiring installation for flaws.

"Do you have any idea how long you have been here?"

"Yes, I learned on my way back from the hospital. It's been eleven months. Without any contact with the outside world I'd lost all track of time. From what I know of ceramics, this operation will take three months or more to complete. By the time we finish this job it will be well over a year without ever seeing a paycheck."

"Ted. I'm keeping track of the number of breakfasts I've had and if my figures are anywhere near right, I've been here over five years."

"Paycheck or no paycheck the sun looked mighty good from my hospital window. Had any thoughts about escaping?"

"Yeah, who hasn't?"

"Have you found a way?"

"I'm not sure. I've been watching those Gray People coming and going as they please. They pass right through the walls like a ghost.

"I watch the scrap containers as they're taken away. If a person could hide in one of them, then you would get pulled to the outside where the scrap is collected. I'm planning to take a container and place it against the wall, climb in and pull electrical scraps over me. The containers are almost full, they will be collected soon, like tonight."

"It's worth a try. But what if it doesn't work and you're caught?"

"I'll be in solitary for a while. I took the precaution of keeping the wiring schematics in my head. I'm willing to risk it."

Sam's plan didn't work. He was placed in solitary for two weeks by Ted's count of the number of times he ate breakfast. Sam's work was too valuable to the company for him to remain off the job for long. His insurance plan paid off. He returned to the electrical department wearing his old orange uniform. That still gave him the freedom to go anywhere in The Shop, but now he had an escort. The same large man who took Ted to and from his room and work stations.

"I think I found another way out."

"How, Sam?"

"In the storage room at the bottom of the wall where it meets the floor. There is a hole that didn't get filled when the building was built. My guess is, it was missed when the foundation was back filled. A little work to make it larger, a person would be able to crawl through it. Don't know where it goes, but measuring with a pole, I don't touch any blockage."

"How would we be able to get in there, Sam? The doors are locked at the end of the day."

"You'll be reassigned to the welding and forge department after the ceramic order is completed, won't you?"

"No. I'll be assigned to the wood working department making gun stocks. Frank wants me back, Mr. Andy told me."

"How long will it take you to complete the job?"

"A week or so if I bust ass."

"Good. It will give me time to arrange something in the foundry that will require your skills of pouring molds. The big forge built into the back wall will put you near the storage room."

"Okay."

"You will have access to the supply room to get whatever the welder needs. I'm in electrical, but some of my tools are kept there. When your day is finished you could tell your watcher you locked the doors to the storage room. Just hang the lock in the hasp so it looks like the doors are locked. He won't take the time to check them for himself and miss his dinner.

"We can try it several times to see if it works. If it does we'll slip out of here some afternoon. We have to do it during the day while we're in the shop. We won't be missed until our watchers came looking for us at the end of the day. By then we'll be long gone."

"Sam, let's not get in any hurry. That way they won't suspect anything."

"You're right. A little longer won't make a difference. If one of us gets a transfer we must go that day if we expect to get out of here alive."

Sam's cryptic comment struck deep in Ted's soul. He knew then the only way they'd be allowed to leave The Shop was to die. His accident was a fluke – it wasn't supposed to have happened. The entire month he was in the hospital he was kept in isolation.

When Sam's watcher came for him at the end of the day Sam was told there was a job coming up in the future, an addition to the building on the outside that needed an electrician, a welder, and a helper.

"You have been chosen to do the electric work. Ted will be the helper for you and the welder. The length of the job depends the three of you. Don't try to drag it out. The Gray People will make the job difficult enough. You will be notified when the job starts. It will take a few days to gather the tools you'll need so they can be moved outside."

"Ted's watcher and the welder's watcher are being told of the job."

While they were eating their last meal of the day his watcher was talking more than Ted had ever heard from him. He kept his head bent over his meal so his moving lips looked like he was eating.

"When the new project is closer to being ready, you're to give Sam and Bill, the welder, any help they need getting their tools together. Place them next to the scrap containers."

The Gray People hadn't bothered Ted or his work after he recognized the crushed shell casings. His watcher had told him about the new job as a helper on the addition. The Gray People had been vandalizing the new addition's construction site, equipment, and supplies.

"We found some of the tools near a sinkhole. After we retrieved what they stole we sent a dozer over to push trash into the hole to fill it in. We hope that will keep them in the hole." Ted took the risk of making a comment.

"You do know that where you have a sinkhole it's likely to be where the roof of a cave that has collapsed. The Gray People may be living in the cave and surviving off of the debris. All you have to do is keep them in the cave."

"How, Ted"?

"If you know where the opening to the cave is, you could go in and blow it up causing a cave-in, which would seal it."

"Are you sure that will work?"

"Fairly sure. A long time ago, they had a similar problem in the coal mines. They were called Tommy Knockers, but they sound the same as these Gray People who are plaguing The Shop."

"Heard of 'em, but what are Tommy Knockers?"

"Real Tommy Knockers are spirits of dead miners who

dwell in the mines, to warn the living miners when trouble is coming. They're known all over the world where deep pit mining is done. Some, just like people, go rogue causing a lot of destruction as well as loss of lives among the miners. Sealing them in abandoned mines is the method most often used to get rid of the bad ones."

"Where do they go?"

"Experts think they're killed or retreat into the crevasses deeper underground near the fires of hell."

"Haven't heard about any caves."

"Since Sam and I've been chosen to work outside, we could look around for an opening as we work. If you could arrange to get some dynamite, we could blow up the cave if we find it, and seal in the Gray People.

"You said you had filled in a sinkhole this morning."

"Yes. It's back in the woods behind the building."

"Could you have it dug out, even though you just had it filled in?"

"I suppose we could. But why?"

"Don't you see? The trash in the sinkhole could be working its way through a cave. If so, there's your cave opening. While it's being dug out, Sam and I can be looking around for another opening."

"When we come for you and Sam tomorrow we'll take you guys outside, so you can get started. I can arrange to send a track hoe to the sinkhole.

"You talk to Sam. Getting the dynamite is the easy part. There is some in a supply shed, for use on the construction site if they hit bedrock. I'll let you know when things are ready."

Ted was so happy he felt like dancing back to his room. A few more days, then freedom! He had a difficult time keeping a smile off his face.

When Sam drifted past his work desk, he took a chance and whispered, "Sam, we're getting out of here."

"How?"

"There's been a lot of trouble from the Gray People disrupting the preparations for the addition construction on the outside. They need our help to eliminate them."

"How soon?"

"Don't know. My watcher said he'd come for us with the stuff we would need.

Three days passed before Ted's watcher appeared in the metals room. It was the middle of the afternoon. He was accompanied by the Waiter, who was wearing a red jumpsuit, the same man who'd first brought Ted into the company.

Once he and Sam were outside the building Ted got the shock of his life. The Waiter gave a slight nod to Bill, the welder, a small oriental with greying hair. Bill spun around and delivered a swift blow to the base of his watcher's neck. The man was dead before he hit the ground.

Ted looked around, not believing his eyes as he got a second shock. He was too stunned to make a sound. His and Sam's watchers were twins!

One of them picked up the body and threw it in the scoop of a huge dozer that was idling near where they stood. Then, together they tilted the dumpster. The Waiter pulled out a suitcase.

He said, "Get in the dumpster and change clothes – fast. It'll be crowded, but you'll make it while I take care of the stiff."

Ted caught sight of him climbing into the cab of the dozer ripping off his jumpsuit.

The Waiter yelled back, "Don't waste time on introductions. Get busy. Do your job and get out. Take the sewer under the road."

Like the others, Ted found a packet of jeans, a T-shirt, and a jacket his size in the suitcase. As the man said – it was tight.

Everyone got a couple of elbows before they managed to change. No one said a word.

Ted had told his watcher how find the cave entrance. He'd said he and Sam would search for it. In a way he'd given his word, though his instinct was to run as if the hounds of hell were on his heels. A given word was the one code he'd ever had to live by. This didn't stop him from looking at the distance woods with longing.

"Come on, Sam. We can start here and go along the wall of the building to the back."

"Ted, how do you know if we can find it?"

"Grew up in cave country.

"We'll work our way back to the hole, under the wall outside of the storage room, looking for a small opening in the ground. If puffs of smoky shadows are coming out of it, then we'll know how the Gray People are getting in and out of the building. When we get to the hole behind the storage room. we'll work our way to the sinkhole near the woods."

They rounded the corner of the building to where the addition was planned. The wall was solid, no windows on the backside of the building. A thirty-foot area had been leveled and covered with asphalt.

There was nothing for them to find. The woods were less than twenty yards beyond the building. Ted estimated he could sprint to them if worst came to worst. He wasn't going back into The Shop.

About midway to the woods, the back end of the track hoe disappeared. The driver had found a new hole by accident. The engine roared as he gave it more fuel. The big machine slowly crawled out of the new hole.

Ted and Sam ran for their lives to the huge machine and hid behind it before looking down into the pit. The Waiter had opened up an entrance to a cave that looked as if it ran under the company buildings.

The Waiter was giving orders fast and furious.

"Ted, you've had experience with explosives. Go ahead with your plan. Get down into the cave, as far as you safely can to set the charges. Take Sam and Bill with you.

"I brought the dynamite with me on this track hoe. When you and Sam finish, come back to The Company. I'll bring the two of you in."

Ted wasn't having any part of that idea. He was out and he was staying out.

"I said I'd blow the cave and I will, but no way am I going back in that building.

"Sam, here's our chance. When it blows, we'll be home free. If there is enough dynamite the reverberations will bring down the buildings."

"I'm with Ted. When this is all over, we may be dead if things don't go right, but I'm free and I'll die if I have to, but I'll still be free."

It was getting dark top-side, but it didn't matter down in the hole. When Ted looked up he could see stars, like he did when he helped his uncle dig a well when he was a kid. It was hard work lacing the sticks of dynamite together. Bill and Sam held powerful flashlights.

Ted felt a drop of water fall on his hand. He noticed he was sweating and shed his jacket. He handed it to Sam.

Sam was sweating too. How long had it been since they'd been hot enough to sweat? He couldn't remember.

51

Sam was nervous about being down under and started talking.

"If I don't make it out, I've got to tell you something. "I'm a undercover federal agent, the Bureau.

"When I stopped in *The Shop's Bar & Grill* I was there investigating a drug and money laundering operation on my first assignment. The Bureau chief thought it was simple setup and had no idea what I walked into. I never got out."

As he worked, Ted could hear Sam's teeth chattering, as if he was cold. There was no time to waste by talking. He needed all his concentration to not blow them out of the hole before all of the charges were set.

"I've never believed in ghosts, until the night I saw the face of one of the Gray People. It was the face of the guy I roomed with during training. I didn't know he had the same assignment. I believe the Gray People are former employees the Company killed – to keep them quiet."

Ted stood up and flexed his cramped legs. They didn't have much time to get out. Bill turned to pick up the bail of fuse line. Sam grabbed him. Ted had seen what the little man had done to the watcher and reached for Sam. Bill didn't move.

Sam screamed, "Who is that Waiter guy?"

"United States Army Intelligence."

"What? Who are you and those two giants?"

"His personal wrecking crews."

Ted gave them both a shove toward the entrance of the cave hole.

"Get out of here fast. We're going to blow The Company straight to hell and back. Once I push the plunger on the box we'll have to run for the woods as fast as we can. It won't take long for the dynamite to go off blowing debris hundreds of yards in all directions."

The twins were waiting above the hole and hauled them out as Ted unrolled the spool of wire. Bill went straight to the Waiter, said something then climbed up into the track hoe. It began a trudging journey toward the woods, taking Sam and the twins with him.

The Waiter stayed behind and helped Ted wind the wires around the terminals.

"Make tracks. When I push the plunger I'm right behind you."

Together they made the edge of the woods, just as the earth ripped open in a huge ball of flame, lighting up the night sky for miles. The six men cut through the woods at a decent jog that was set by the Waiter. He seemed to know the paths. Ted knew what the man was doing. He was conserving their strength in case they really had to run for it.

Sirens were cutting through the night like the blasting force cut through the cave. Ted's long-unused legs, though he estimated he was the youngest by ten or fifteen years, were beginning to feel it. Sam was lagging behind when the Waiter called a halt.

"Okay…I'm with the Bureau. You…are with the Army. But…is Ted?"

"An innocent bystander who happened along at the wrong time. Are you alright, son?"

"Yes, Sir." Ted answered automatically to the man's overpowering air of command.

The Waiter pointed to the twins. "Thanks. Go home in different directions so no one will connect you. There's going to be hordes of people around here asking questions you don't want to answer."

They shook hands and the twins vanished among the trees.

"Bill, help Sam get to the nearest state police station. Don't use local people – we haven't sorted out the riffraff yet.

"Come on, Ted. I'll find a way to get you home. Your adventuring days are finished. We'll leave the Gray People to their revenge."

~ ~ ~

Ted was sitting in a McDonald's, in a small mid-western town when Sam with a man who was obviously a cop, walked in and joined him.

"Sam Reynolds you know. I'm Curtis Colton, State Police. A friend asked us to come and thank you for your help. He instructed me to give you this."

The officer handed Ted a thick envelope.

"It's clean money you earned working for The Company. They hope it will help until you are able to find a job that isn't so dangerous. It's cash, don't bother to count it, especially not here. Get yourself a lockbox at a bank and then count it. The man you helped has never worked cheap. If you have to report it for taxes, it is up to Sam. He's the Fed."

"Ted, I was investigating the disappearance of several town officials that had told the rest of the board members they were going out to THE COMPANY for lunch. That was the last time they were ever seen. It was thought the rest of the board were getting kickbacks for keeping quiet about *The Shop's Bar & Grill* and The Company that was connected with the restaurant."

Sam reached in his pocket and pulled out one of the ceramic pieces Ted had made in The Shop.

"This survived the blast. I thought you might like to have it for a souvenir. These little beauties were filled with cocaine and distributed through carnivals to carefully selected buyers.

"Shortly, the Company will pass their last funny money and dirty drugs. We'll never know where or how many of the damn things made their way into public hands. Thanks to you, The Shop is out of business."

Sam and the State Police officer walked out of Ted's life and he never saw them again. There had been enough money in the envelope for him to purchase a small machine shop, with living expenses until he got started.

Ted loved to sit at his special table by the window, at the *Stargazer Cafe*, eating biscuits and gravy with scrambled eggs and watching the sun come over horizon.

He had his coffee and a cigarette while reading the early morning paper about the fallout from the collapse of The Company. No mention was made of the Army guys or the Gray People – it was if they vanished or had never existed. Ted knew his newspaper was as close as he ever, wanted to get to the real thing again.

The yearlong investigations that were reported in the paper read almost like a novel you picked up in an airport.

The police found a huge meat cooler below the restaurant packed with boxes of money and cocaine. Street value placed the stash at well over five hundred million dollars. It was the largest drug and money laundering operation the world had ever seen for the time. Arrests were made in many places across the United States as well as in Europe.

# NIGHT SCREAMS

Barbara and Lester Lewis' children Mary, Sue, and Henry wanted to convince their parents to retire from farming because of their age. The farm covered close to eight hundred acres. The kids believed a golf course was a better use for the land than hardscrabble farming.

The dilapidated house was in desperate need of repairs. Lester's ancient Farmall tractor was so old it cost more and more each year to keep it in working condition. The clothes they wore in the fields would have made better rags for polishing the wood stove.

The farm was a good ten miles from town, on a narrow one lane road that ran along the edge of a bluff above Carr Creek, in Ono County. It was hazardous to drive in the summer, let alone in the winter after snow or freezing rain.

The road surface was made of crushed gravel that crumbled from the cliffs. The roadbed got narrower each time the edge gave way. The valley below was lush with green fields that could be watered by Carr Creek during dry spells.

In late October of 1969, the wind began blowing in the valley before it climbed the bluff between the hills. That night, Lester had a run in with spooks he'd never forget to his dying day.

He was jerked out of bed in the middle of the night as the loud screams of a person in dire pain echoed through the hills.

Abruptly, they stopped as if they were too great a burden to be carried on the back of the wind as it climbed the hill.

Lester grabbed his shotgun and ran out into the yard in his long johns figuring it was a catamount near the barn making those unearthly sounds.

His Red Nosed Beagle didn't raise his head as Lester sped past him to the barnyard. Strange. Dubber was normally on his feet barking his head off if a squirrel ran across the yard.

All was quiet in the barn: cows munching on bits of hay showing no sign of being disturbed, chickens roosting in the henhouse without a feather fluttering. It was as if none of the animals had heard the screams that rousted him from his warm bed.

He returned to the house where he found Barbara sitting in front the fire she'd built in the fireplace. It was the only means of heat in the old farmhouse, except for the kitchen range.

"Thank you for building the fire, Barb. It's what we need. It's gotten chilly outside."

"I didn't build the fire, I thought you did."

"No, not me. You're the only one here, aren't you?"

"Lester, you got up before I did. When I came in the kitchen the fire was burning and the coffee was starting to perk."

"Woman. I didn't start that fire. I ran straight out to the barn. Look, I'm still in my long johns. Didn't even take time to dress. Figured a big cat was after the cow as she has come fresh."

"Have some of the coffee you didn't make." Her voice was thick with scorn. "Sit by that fire you didn't start to warm up. You must be chilled to the bone as long as you were outside."

Lester reached for his mug of coffee. He took his brew black and strong. Barb liked cream and sugar in hers. They sat by the fire, in their rocking chairs, enjoying the coffee while each one wondered what had happened. They avoided mentioning the fire or the coffee as if the presence of something they could not explain would shatter their trust in each other.

Lester fell asleep. He was jolted awake by a hot foot. He had slid down in his chair. This put his left foot too close to the fire. His boot was smoking. He jumped around the room yelling, "My foot is on fire!"

He stuck his foot in the bucket of water they kept next to the fireplace for safety.

A commotion arose in the kitchen as his boot sizzled. Jerking his foot from it, he ran to the kitchen.

The table and benches were floating in the air, turning in a slow circle above the sink. No one was in the kitchen. Barbara had gone back to bed.

The heavy pieces stopped and fell to the floor with a loud crash. It seemed to Lester as if whatever was causing the furniture to float had seen him in the doorway and fled out the back door.

He ran after whatever it was, but stopped on the porch. Brilliant sunlight showered a golden glow in his yard, but nothing was there that he could see.

Lester scanned the slide road down through the holler between the ridges to the creek, where he trapped fish to eat and sell in town. A light breeze blew up from the creek. As he walked down the slide road the wind grew stronger. It became a struggle to move against the battering force. He walked bent over like the old man he refused to admit to being.

Trash was blowing around in the air and through the trees as if a garbage truck had dumped its load.

Loud voices followed by piercing screams were coming up from the creek. When Lester reached the creek he discovered his fish traps busted on the bank with dead and dying fish scattered through the rocks. His catch was ruined as well as his plans to sell the fish. He had promised Barbara a new bonnet. He hastily gathered the remains of his dream together and dumped it in the creek to be washed away.

An eerie silence fell over the sheltered cove as he worked. He could not hear even a cricket chirping in the grass. He started back up the slide road, scratching his head and mumbling to himself.

"I can't understand what's happening."

Lester hadn't gone far up the steep slide road when a strong gust of wind picked him up, carried him to the top, then dumped him on the back porch of the cabin in his rocking chair.

He was sitting with his face in his hands, shaking his head and mumbling when Barbra came out on the porch, looking for him.

"Lester, are you okay?"

"No woman, I'm not. I don't understand."

"Understand what, Lester? What are you talking about?"

"You didn't see them."

"See what?"

"The table and benches in the kitchen, flying around in mid-air."

"Lester Lewis, have you lost your mind? Puncheon tables don't fly."

"The fierce wind, like a tornado, with loud voices and screams, howling like a banshee up the slide road. Trash blowing through the trees and, not to mention – how it picked me up when I started home from the creek and dropped me in this chair. You didn't hear that?"

"No. You were dreaming."

"I don't understand, Barb. What happened to me?"

"You'll be alright. You've had too much to drink."

Lester's temper got the best of him. She always harped on his taking a nip now and then. She hadn't believed him about the screams that pitched him into this nightmare. Now she was harking back to his taking a sip on special occasions.

"Woman, I haven't had anything stronger than that swill you call coffee."

"I told you that shine you make back in the hills would rot your brain some day. What little you have left."

"Speaking of brew. I'm going to the shed for my jug. I don't want to hear anything more about it when I come back. I aim to sit right on this porch and have a few snorts. Then take a nap."

"Lester, why don't you get the mail before you get so loaded you won't be able to walk."

"I'll drive down later to the mail box. Too far to walk."

Lester's nap lasted almost four hours. When he rousted himself from his slumbers, the jug was in one hand and the mail in the other.

He almost slid out of the chair – the shock was so great.

"Barb, come out here! Did you get the mail?"

"No, I told you to get it before you got loaded."

"Well, I don't remember leaving this chair, but here's the mail."

"Bring it in instead of sitting out there talking nonsense. It's getting on toward dark. Supper is on if you're up to eating it. If not I'll feed it to the hogs."

Lester managed to get up from his chair and stagger into the kitchen.

"Dammit woman, I've told you. I wasn't drinking. Look. The jug out on the back porch is still corked. The seal isn't broken. Right where I left it when I came in for supper."

He remembered he'd taken the jug into the bedroom. How did it get out on the porch by his rocker?

"Barb, I think it's the kids trying to drive me out of my mind so they can put me in a nuthouse and get the farm."

"No! No, Lester, the children love you. They just want what's best for you. Next, you'll be doubting me."

"I know what I saw."

"You had a bad dream. It's all in your mind. An ugly dream that never happened. Think about what time of the year it is."

"What time of the year…?"

"It's the last day of October. Lester, does that ring a bell?"

Lester shuddered as he heard the back door creak open to let in a putrid odor of tainted, rotting fish blow through the kitchen.

He heard the voices.

"Les…ter. We've got your number."

# BEHIND THE DOOR

Faith, our maid, never cleans behind my door.

When the door is opened from the hall and pushed back against the wall, it leaves a dark hidden space. It's my size, shaped like my tricycle was before Billy put it under the back of Daddy's truck. Daddy smashed it flat when he backed out of the driveway.

The space is my secret place – a fort against invaders.

Billy's bigger than me. He pinches me when we're out in the backyard and Mother's not looking. Calls me a baby if I yell.

He pushed me out of the swing. Told Mother I fell. I broke my arm and had to go to the hospital. Daddy made me a small swing for my Bear, just like the one we have in the backyard. He said the big one was too dangerous until I grew to be Billy's size.

The little swing fits behind my door in the secret place.

I hid Bear with it behind the door so Billy won't take him and smash Bear's face with Daddy's hammer, like he did my monkey.

Billy told Mother I did it.

He is mean. I don't like him. When I can, I hide from him behind the door. He bangs into my room and flings the door back against the wall. I stay very still and put my hand over Bear's mouth so he won't squeal. Billy can't see me in my corner. I'm safe.

He put spiders in my bed. The bumps, where they bit me swelled up. They made me sick. I had to go to the doctor and get shots.

Billy dumped my goldfish down the toilet. He told Mother Iffy, our cat, ate it. Iffy hates him. He pulls her tail if he catches her. I can't jump to the top of the refrigerator and hiss like she does. I wish I could. Even Billy can't reach that high.

I cry myself to sleep after a bad-bad day. I put my head under the covers so Mother won't hear me. Once Billy tripped me and ran away when I fell in a puddle and skinned my face. Mother put a paste on it that stung and burned.

Tonight, I hear a giggle and feel a thump on my leg. I sit up. The corners of my room are dark, except for a moonbeam falling through the window. It bends and twists like the tube where we go to get burgers. Mother lets me slide down it if Daddy is there to catch me.

Two little men, the size of Bear, tumble out of the round light on my quilt. I watch them. Their ears are pointed like Iffy's. They bend their heads, put crooked fingers behind their peaky ears and push them forward to listen. Then they race back up the beam to slide again – over and over. I want to join them, but their tube is too small for me.

The moonbeam moves and is gone, taking the little men with it. Iffy stalks into my room, hissing like she does when she is mad at Billy. She takes a swipe at the stray moonbeam on the floor and jumps on my bed. She squiggles under the covers to curl up beside me. Then she pushes against my tummy, which tickles, with her paws as she stretches.

School starts for Billy. We go with him the first day. Mother pulled me, with Billy's book bag in the red wagon. Billy won't ride. He stalks like a mad dog in front of us, all the way. He makes fun of me and says riding is for babies.

Mother is talking to his teacher. He gets his book bag out of the wagon and hits me with the strap. It hurts and leaves a red mark on my arm. He tells her I'm crying because I'm not old enough to go to school.

Mother leaves him with his teacher. I hope he never comes back. We stop for ice cream. It's nice now that Billy isn't here. I have Mother all to myself. She said he'd come home after school on a yellow bus. We'd go to meet him at the corner with the red wagon.

When it rains I have to stay inside. I don't mind. Billy isn't home during the school day. My friends of the night, stay and play with me, behind the door where it's dark, even during the day. My friends don't like Billy. Like me, they run and hide so he can't find them. They call him a goat. I call him a goat one afternoon when we met his bus. He kicks me and leaves a blue mark on my leg.

Mother and Daddy don't know I get up when they're in bed. I like the night when Billy is asleep and can't hurt me.

My friends come at night, the house is so quiet I can hear the grandfather clock ticking in the hall. We slip downstairs like little mice, they scurry inside the clock case and make it chime by swinging on the chains.

The tip of the clock's hands look like my space behind the door. Their pointed ends are sharp as when you hold your finger up to the wind.

They spot Billy's book bag by the door and want to explore. With my help on the zipper, we get it open. Billy's box of colored crayons spill out and roll across the floor.

It's funny to see as my little friends hoist them up like tall candles in a parade of colors. Then I giggle as they carry each crayon like a flagpole and topple it over the side of the box. Some are broken and bent, but we get them back in the box.

Billy tells Mother I'd been in his book bag and played with his crayons. She laughs at him. He gives me the evil eye.

One night, a white bottle rolls out of the bag. I pull the big orange end. My friends take turns jumping on the orange cap and twirling around, like on a jungle gym, until it pops off. A sticky white glob oozes out in the crayon box.

We get the top back on the bottle and stuff it back in Billy's book bag.

When Billy gets home from school, he is hopping mad. Tells Mother a kid at school dumped his bottle of glue in his crayons. Ruined them. She gets him to admit he may have been careless and put it away with a loose cap. I put my hand over my mouth so they won't hear me snicker.

I tell my special friends. We laugh and laugh. We roll on the floor kicking our feet in the air. Getting back at Billy is fun.

Billy never does anything bad according to Daddy. He doesn't have to take time-outs like I do when I lose my temper and cry when my brother hits me.

Daddy doesn't have time to tell me stories before I go to sleep. He has to stay in the kitchen with Billy, helping him with a school project. They're building a tiny town on a board and painting each building a different color.

It's a perfect place for my friends to play, just their size. I watch them run from building to building, slamming doors. They knock over the water tower and go sliding though the water leaving red, blue, and yellow streaks through the streets.

The next morning, Billy races downstairs to take his project to school. Mother says he stepped on one of the little cars and fell. He lands on the project, knocking it to the floor. When Daddy picks it up, it's ruined, the little houses soggy and smashed.

We have a bowl of corn flakes with bananas and milk before we go to bed. One night, Mother leaves the box on the counter in the kitchen. Iffy knocks it to the floor. I pick it up – it's almost as tall as I am. I tug and pull to get it up the stairs to Billy's room. My friends push from behind to help me move the big box. We creep in through his door, making no noise except the slip, slip sound of the box as I drag it across the floor. I tilt the box over Billy's shoes.

My friends climb up the sides of the shoes. They jump up and down, crushing the flakes to fine crumbs. The next morning Billy wakes me up, screaming mad.

Snow is fun. The cold bites my nose. Mother takes us to the big hill across from our house. Billy has his sled. She lets me ride in her huge dishpan pulled by a rope. We watch from the hill as he slides down the hill, past the fish pond. For three sunny days we play in the snow until, on the third day Billy's sled sails down the hill. It flies off the path into the pond. Billy sinks under the ice.

Mother screams and leaves me on the hill. She runs down the hill. People keep her from running into the pond after him. The fire department comes and get him out. It is too late.

They take him to the hospital. He doesn't come home. Mother holds me and cries. Billy is never coming home. He went to a funeral home.

Billy is dead.

Later, Daddy says the runner of the sled was dented and bent as if it hit a rock, throwing him off course into the pond.

They put him in a box and dump the box in the ground. We stand beside the hole, in the cold. I throw a smelly flower on the box and watch the dirt cover the box.

Mother and Daddy are sad, but I'm glad. They hug me. Now, Daddy tells me stories before I go to sleep. He asks me if I miss Billy. I say yes. Daddy doesn't know Billy can't hurt me if he's dead. I take Bear out of my secret place and put him on my bed. Billy can't smash in his face with Daddy's hammer. You can't come back from being dead. I hear a lady tell that to Mother. Next summer, I'll be big enough to use the swing in the backyard by myself.

In the dark, I hold Iffy and Bear and mourn for my special friends who don't visit anymore.

Faith cleans behind the door and finds the hammer.

# Ghost Winds

Summer had come and gone in Ono County. The days grew shorter as the sun settled lower and lower in the western sky.

The leaves changed earlier and faster than anyone could remember: a sign of an early and bad winter. At the rate the leaves were changing and dropping, the trees would be stripped before the first strong storm blew up from the lower end of the valley from the river bottom.

By Halloween, a wintery chill settled in the valley. The first heavy snow fell before Thanksgiving, which came early this year leaving a month until Christmas. A few days later four inches of ice and snow pelted the upper valley, closing schools and downing power lines as the heavy accumulation took its toll.

Down at the lower end of the valley, bellowing gusts and howls could be heard as trees bent and buckled when fierce winds blew out of the north, over the mountains. Violent cracks, like heavy artillery bombardment, bounced across the valley as trunks split or limbs broke under heavy loads.

Old timers, who huddled around the pot-bellied stove at Osborne's General Store, near the crossroad, about fifteen miles between Clydesville and the upper valley of Ono County matched tales of other winters. All agreed this one was a humdinger as it had come early. Each took a turn plucking feathers from a covey of quail Jass Dingus found frozen to the ground under a stand of blackberry bushes.

Old Harold, though he was past ninety, could still cook-up a tasty mess of birds in that old iron chicken fryer Young Oz kept in the back room.

The town below grew colder as the temperature on top of the mountain dropped well past zero. Each new blast of Arctic air dumped layers of snow through the valley and on the mountains. Deadman's Creek became thick with slush, like a chocolate milkshake. All said it would freeze over if the intense cold continued. A heavy fish kill would poison the waters. The brown trout wouldn't return to spawn.

Folks at the upper end of the valley claimed they'd seen clouds of green light drift through the treetops. While strange sights were seen by the people in the valley. These took on the shape of people, as they floated in and out among the trees, following the creek up the holler. Their features became more distinct as they appeared in the cold air near the top of the mountain. There, they looked like people who had lived and died in the valley.

Some claimed they could identify the features of those who'd died during the war in other lands or people who had moved away. Families who lived on the mountain at Buck Run came to believe they were spirits who had come home to visit for the holidays, as kinfolks always did.

Ominously, as the end of November drew nearer, rumblings were heard from deep within the earth. The screams and other sounds of torment, carried on fierce winds, became louder. Apparitions multiplied as if End of the Road Cemetery was belching up every coffin.

At night, the wind blew so hard the dry snow drifted, making it look as if a fresh snow had fallen. Worried eyes watched new footprints lead to some storefronts, then disappear into the night before people were out stirring. Tire tracks, glittering in the moonlight, went nowhere in the drifted snow.

Ono County was justly proud of the two snow removal trucks they had managed to obtain from a state sale. They were old and cranky, but under Al Simpson's expert care they came to life to clear the roads and spread cinders over icy bridges.

This year since the first pre-Thanksgiving snows the frequent blasts of snow and ice had strained the endurance of the drivers to the point they only worked highway 1027, which was the main road running through the county. Citizens and farmers in outlying areas had to shift for themselves.

The three members of the road department reported to work around 3:00 am to start the plows and let them warm up before loading the hoppers with a mixture of cinders, road salt, and sand. Normally, after the huge diesel engines lumbered to life the snowplows were on the roads about an hour later.

However, when the road crew arrived at the maintenance garage, after another night of blowing snow, they discovered their trucks where gone. What happened to the equipment they'd parked the night before? Al Simpson rang Ono County Judge Green at home, to report the missing county equipment.

By the time the judge got to his office in Clydesville, frantic calls were coming in. The snowplows were blocking both ends of the main road leading into town.

Judge Green trudged through the deep drifts that filled the open spaces between buildings to where one of the trucks was parked. There he met the angry callers who had taken shelter in the Kricket Kafe, outside of town on 1027. Together they investigated the area around the stolen truck. They found footprints indicating that the driver vacated the truck with the engines still running.

When Judge Green got back to his office Tom Clement of the *Chronicle* was on the phone demanding to know what had happened, as he had been unable to get past one of the trucks for his breakfast.

The judge called the council members, as well as the entire maintenance department to his office to see if anyone knew why the trucks were hindering traffic instead of helping it.

At the end of two hours of wrangling, the only solution they could all agree on was that it must have had something to do with the green lights, the apparitions that had been seen, or the noises and screams heard going up the mountain. It was an idea that satisfied no one, least of all Judge Green who said it made him look like a fool to be attributing the hijacked trucks to spooks.

The meeting was adjourned.

When the drivers got back to their garage they found the trucks parked at the side of the building with motors running and full tanks of fuel. A note was taped to the steering wheel of each truck proclaiming the truck had been serviced and was ready to plow the roads. It looked to them like a prank, pulled by drunks who didn't have enough sense to stay home on a cold night.

The judge was called and informed of the new development. The crew locked up and went home to catch up on missed sleep before they were scheduled to report back to work.

The next morning was like the day before. The blowing snow had been pushed to each end of the main road. The trucks were, again, blocking the road. There was no evidence of the regular drivers ever being in the trucks. Nor were there any signs they'd left their trucks and walked away, leaving them where they stopped.

That evening, after being called names by Judge Green, Al Simpson locked the trucks in the shed and bolted the big gates to the yard. As a safety precaution he took all the keys and went home to get some sleep after two nights of fighting phantoms. Al had the forethought of taking his phone off the hook as he had no intention of trying to explain to Tom Clement, for the paper, what was happening in his yard.

In the meantime, Clydesville went ahead with decorating the square for the Christmas season. December first marked the beginning of Advent and the annual lighting of the tree, in the park under the shelter of the bandstand. People from all over came into town for the event. The stores held evening hours as did the courthouse where the ladies' auxiliary fed hot chocolate and fruitcake to members of the high school band.

Evergreen branches, trimmed from trees, were collected from the Christmas tree lot operated by the Masons. The wreaths were assembled and decorated by church volunteers. Some of the volunteers pitched in to help Elroy Harris and Lon Chambers hang the wreaths on the light poles around the square.

After the hanging of the wreaths, the lights and the sounds in the hills became more frequent. The sounds began to sound like Christmas music and the lights resembled the northern lights. They could be northern lights even so far south, if the air was clear enough.

The lights and the music did not happen on the same nights. Some nights neither one occurred. On the nights the lights floated across the sky there were severe snowstorms on top of the mountain. If the wind were blowing, it would blow the snow down into the town. As the crews plowed the snow, more snow filled in behind what was just moved aside. The storms lasted as long as the lights floated in the sky over the mountain top, sometimes for several days.

The street lights and the lights on the wreaths began coming on and going off at odd times, even during the day. It was weird to watch as sometimes the lights were on together, yet at other times they alternated. The town's people didn't know what was happening. It was unsettling, different from anything they'd ever known in their lives.

Was there a connection between the lights in the sky above the mountains to the streetlights and the colored lights on the wreaths? The preachers proclaimed it was God's way of heralding the coming of the birth of his son or the end of the world when all would face his judgment.

The council met on the fifteenth of the month to close the books on the previous month's financial operations. Normally, the business session was short and within half an hour the members could go home to supper. Not this time.

Two boutique shops that catered to the summer tourist trade but refused to carry the handcrafted items from the people up in the hills, demanded time to speak of their concerns. Judge Green granted their request as he'd welcomed their store openings as an added means of new revenue without raising taxes.

They found disturbing things had been happening overnight in their stores. When they arrived to open in the morning, they were unable to unlock their doors without calling a locksmith to cut new keys. Their lights were turned off when the stores closed at the end of their business day, yet in the mornings the lights were on. They knew they'd opened the master switch before locking the door.

The unusual thing the lone sheriff's deputy, who patrolled at night, reported was the lights in the two stores kept going off and on. He'd checked and found all the stores to be secure.

Also, the boutique stores' owner's reported looking in the windows to see their merchandise had been moved and some shelves had been swept bare. They even continued to complained of the "tacky" homemade wreaths and that the council had not purchased their plastic wreaths, never noticing that the members had closed their ears to these concerns.

Judge Green studied his tree through the glass doors of the chamber. Didn't these outsiders understand? Ono County was steeped in traditions and treasured its past. His family was gone, so each year he brought the ornaments they had collected during their lifetimes to the courthouse to share his memories of Christmas past with all who entered.

As the days passed, people began speculating about these happenings and if the strange things at the county maintenance garage could be related. Naysayers proclaimed the strange lights and sounds that were coming from the hills had put a curse on the town. They rang Tom Clement with their far-fetched ideas to get their name in the paper.

At the end of the week the shifting lights stopped. The heavy clouds that shrouded Ono County opened to a bright blue sky. The reflection of the sun off the deep snow was intense. The frost flakes danced in the cold air producing a glittering field, where to look upon it blinded the beholder.

Grace Dell, the most renowned saintly teacher who'd ever lived, was walking across the park. She reached the bandstand, paused to admire the tree and nativity scene sheltered there, under the octagonal roof. She turned away, waved to Judge Green, who was standing in his window, and continued on her way.

When she reached the spot in the park where each year on Twelfth Night all the wreaths were dismantled and burned, she burst into flame.

It was only an instant, witnessed by two men. The flames shot high into the clear sky, then shrank to disappear into the blinding snow.

Judge Green watched it from his office window and screamed. Tom Clement saw it from his office in the *Chronicle* building. He raced down the steps, jerking the slide on his ancient Speed Graphic Press Camera. Judge Green arrived from the courthouse as Tom Clement rapidly snapped exposures, but never published the pictures. They were too heinous for public viewing. Neither man would ever fully trust his own eyes for the rest of his life.

At their feet lay part of one of Miss Dell's legs, her sturdy shoe still in place. As they watched in horror, it began to shrivel and disappear into the snow as if she had never existed. The only evidence of her being were the greeting cards she'd been carrying fluttering away on the wind. Grace Dell had disappeared in a fountain of fire.

Their eyes met across a divide of years, disbelief and fear, that bound them to secrecy. No one had seen their panicked run across the park. Who would believe them?

As they stood recovering from deep shock, they were little boys again who'd suffered from twisted ears, fingernail pinched necks and ruler smacked palms, who, like others paid lip service to a false reputation of a classroom tyrant.

Tom Clement walked back to the *Chronicle*, his mind was busy writing the story he would print when someone reported to him that Miss Dell had not returned from her annual winter holiday. He knew Judge Green would never mention what they'd seen. He'd taken too hard a ribbing about the "spooks" that started the snow trucks.

Tom Clement couldn't help smiling. He was remembering the night before when he'd watched the movie, *The Wizard of Oz* with his grandson, Stevie, who had been too quiet and solemn since a tragic boating accident claimed his mother during the summer. Stevie had laughed and clapped when the wicked witch shriveled up and disappeared in flames, much like what his grandfather had just seen.

As soon as the snow stopped and streets in town were cleared it didn't take long for people to get out and about. The merchants were glad to see customers in the stores as Christmas was getting closer and business had been slack.

People from Buck Run, the tiny enclave on the mountain, were able to get into town by late afternoon, but avoided the boutiques who'd refused to carry their crafts. They decorated with homemade ornaments, candles, and lanterns.

The next three days were busy ones for the local merchants as farmers and those who lived in outlying areas were able to use tractors to plow their own roads.

Carstairs Feed and Grain was busy, way into the night as farmers hauled their corn into the mill to be ground for stock feed, and laid in other supplies. Three weeks of being marooned in early winter made them extra cautious to be prepared against later storms. With them came the stories that had been generated around Osborne's potbellied stove during the siege.

Old Harold Osborne had enjoyed telling the story of the strange candy that eventually destroyed the little town of Nome on the other side of the mountains.

Stella Owens and Betsy Parks entered the story while he was yarning. They had returned to Ono County from the coal camps of northeastern Pennsylvania after their husbands were killed in a mining accident, along with twelve other men. They'd taken up an old farm out near Miss Edith Bradley's place where they raised chickens and goats and sold eggs and cheese.

They had been shopping in the feed store and overheard Alvin Carstairs talking to another farmer and joined in when asked about their husbands. They explained that rogue tommy-knockers were believed to have been the cause of the accident where their husbands had been killed.

The farmer left to pick up his wife at Parson's Furniture where she was buying a recliner. While he was waiting for her to finish her purchase, he retold the story he'd heard in the feed store. After they left Mildred Parsons called Louise Bidwell, next door, and told her about the tommy-knockers.

The tale of the tommy-knockers reached Tom Clement as he was locking the *Chronicle* door to go home for supper. It didn't help matters that the person relaying the story was a known town drunk who saw visions at every turn. He was still shaken by the grisly photographs he'd developed and locked away in his safe. A lifetime of being a reporter, who accepted nothing that wasn't supported by fact had been shaken to the core.

After supper, Tom Clement was watching Stevie carefully lift each package from under the tree, study it, and then replace it. He'd done the same thing when he was Stevie's age. The wonder of the gaily wrapped package wasn't of the gift itself, but the mystery of trying to figure out what was hidden by the paper.

Christmas was a time for remembering. He thought of his own grandfather and a walk they'd taken through End of the Road Cemetery, where the dead had been buried since the first settlers came into the area. Some of the graves went back to the late seventeen hundreds. The original name, Flowing River Cemetery, had been lost in time.

Tom Clement's sense of humor kicked into gear at the double meaning of the common name. It was located at the end of a long road with nothing past it but steep cliffs and open sky.

His grandfather had been trying to teach him some of the history of his home through the people who'd lived and died there. He had pointed to a group of sunken graves on the far side. Their markers were long gone, but he mentioned they were miners who'd been killed in a bizarre accident before the turn of the century.

Tom Clement knew the old Shamrock and Lucky Lady mines had closed on the eve of World War I, now swallowed deep under the waters of the man-made lake. If memory served him right they were located on the very western edge of the county not far from where Stevie's mother died, in an area of frequent boating accidents.

*Tommy-Knockers* – that's where he'd heard the term. His grandfather had told him his grandfather had written a story about them in the old *Banner*, as the paper was called in the early days.

Betty Clement wasn't surprised to see her husband get up from his chair, kiss Stevie goodnight, and put on his overcoat. He'd been in a deep study all evening, hardly noticing his supper. She knew he was headed back to the paper, to dig around in the morgue for an old story that was plaguing him.

The *Chronicle's* morgue housed a copy of every paper the Clement family had ever published, going back over a hundred years. His father, Tom Senior, had the precious volumes bound in sturdy buckram bindings with gold lettering on the spines indicating the year and name of the paper at the time. The precious pages were soft and crumbled if not handled carefully. A long, tall tilt-top table with a strong lip ran down the center of the room for holding the heavy tomes.

The room smelt of printer's ink and of the sulphur powder used to combat silverfish, which were a bane if an infestation was allowed to start. The room was kept warm and dry for this reason.

Starting with the first volume and working forward page by page he would stop to admire the crispness of the print when the handset type was new. The old flattop press produced a fine image, though the print would tend to blur if it was screwed down too tight.

He found the story in the 1883 volume of the *Banner* and began to read the simple story.

> *"Tommy-knockers were ghostly spirits that traveled from place to place through caves and could appear in any cave or come out through any opening they could find. One function was to warn deep pit miners of impending disasters so they would have time to get out of the mines.*

> *"The stories of their existence had been passed down through the ages, but were most prevalent in Cornwall, a section of England where tin mines existed back to the time of Jesus. Tradition held that as a young boy, Jesus had visited the tin mines with his uncle, Joseph of Armethia.*

> *"The stories go that the tommy-knockers followed the miners across the ocean and took up residence in the coal mines of Pennsylvania. Then, later followed the miners over the mountains into Kentucky to wreak havoc in the mines."*

The article went on for several pages, more as an editorial cautioning readers not to jump to conclusions and not to panic in light of the recent disaster. The mine owners were investigating and would report back through the paper of their findings.

Tom Clement searched for later articles, but tommy-knockers were never mentioned again, nor was there any report of the findings of an investigation. An old story to be passed around Osborne's Grocery on cold days.

He had no answers. Were the lights above the mountain and the strange behavior of man-made lights caused by firestorms on the sun, which disrupted radio communications? Who had moved the snow plows from the county garage? Were the rumblings from deep in the earth an early sign of an impending earthquake? What caused Miss Dell to disappear in a fountain of flame?

What was the old newspaper adage that hung on the wall behind his grandfather's desk?

*When the facts and myths disagree – print the myths.*

When Tom came out of the *Chronicle* building he was surprised to see it was so late. The town clock atop the courthouse was chiming 3:00 am. It was Christmas morning and he hadn't even noticed.

Judge Green was standing by his tree. Easy to see through the glass doors of the courthouse, reliving times of the past.

The streets were peaceful and quiet. The colored lights on the wreaths and the tree in the park glowed soft and steady. It was time to go home, grab a few hours of sleep and make some new memories of his own.

# LAST TRAIN

I love trains and have since I was a little boy who followed a favorite cousin, the dispatcher, out of the station house to hand messages attached to a long pole, up to the engineer. As they left the siding on the journey west, the fireman would always give two pulls on the sharp whistle as if to say, 'Thanks. See you next time.'

Those childhood thrills began my romance with trains as I've watched passenger cars being replaced by long strings of freight cars, loaded with trailers that would be hitched to cabs of eighteen-wheelers, then hauled to destinations far from the rails.

I know the freight trains are vital to our transportation system, but long rows of black gold from far off mountains that snake around the curves hold no mystique for a traveler. What glamour is there in knowing they will later be switched to small engines to haul their prehistoric cargo to power hydroelectric plants far from their origin. This is mundane commercialism, when stacked against the mystery of a man and woman meeting on a train to explore an unknown destiny.

My name is Tray Stevens, which doesn't mean much in the annals of time. Maybe I've waited too late to make my life count and begin a family. I don't regret those early years, but now my life has taken a new turn.

Nora is soon to be my wife. There's an old song, It Only Takes a Moment. That's how it was for me. The first time I saw her coming down the stairs of a hotel I fell, literally at her feet. Not the most auspicious beginning of an affair, but a sprained ankle got me her phone number.

Winter passed into spring before she agreed to meet me for coffee in a little bistro near the park. It became our place, always in the middle of the afternoon, when it wasn't crowded. She worked evenings and nights.

My lovely, lovely Nora, who turned the heads of a few passing strangers when she walked in with her face hidden behind huge, dark glasses and her red-blonde hair wrapped in a scarf under a large floppy hat.

Our time together was precious. I was finishing the final research for an article on the recently discovered early train engines discovered resting on the floor of Chesapeake Bay. The railway museum had offered a small fellowship for the publicity from my self-indulgence.

I rearranged my work time to fit her available hours. In the mornings I fulfilled the obligations of my grant, then did my digging through their uncataloged archives and did my writing late at night after closing time. The Board of

Trustees was delighted with my request because I served as an unofficial night watchman, thus saving them the expense of hiring another person.

Late one night an insistent pounding on the museum's front door caught my attention. I rushed from the tiny cavern of an office and looked through a small pane of glass beside the door.

Nora was huddled in the shadows of the porch. Her head turning back and forth in jerky movements, searching the deserted street.

I was all thumbs as I couldn't get the locks opened fast enough to get to her. I grabbed her up in my arms and carried her into the museum. Her dress was ripped. I placed her on a display case to the side of the entrance and reached for the light switch.

Her frantic voice stopped me. "No! Don't turn on the lights. He may have followed me."

"What happened?"

I tried to hold her, but she pulled away as if she was afraid of me.

"I was mugged."

"We must call the police."

"No. I'm all right."

To prove it she slid down off the case to stand. She was wobbly and reached out for me as from the museum's front window, a silhouette of a man fell on the floor beside us, then disappeared like a malignant shadow.

Her fingernails dug into my arm.

"Please. Hide me."

"The office. Can you stoop down? The cases will hide us."

We stole around tall cases to the far back corner of the building, feeling our way in the dim glow of streetlights. I'd left the office door open, the greenish glow of the computer screen filling the room.

Once we were safely inside I pushed the door closed with my foot, stood up and turned on the overhead light. The office space was small, packed with bookshelves and filing cabinets, leaving just enough space to turn sideways to get around to the desk.

Nora lay on the floor with her face turned toward a bookcase.

I touched her shoulder. Moving slowly, she turned on her side.

Her face was a mess. She bent her head away from me to hide the cut lip and bruises that were turning black. What was left of the dress she worn was fancy, the kind women wore to cocktail parties.

A small, silver colored purse hung around her neck. A red circle ran around her neck as if the strap had been used to choke her.

"Please turn out the light. He'll see it. He knows I came in one of these buildings."

"Nora, he can't see the light. There are no windows in this room."

She looked up and around as if checking before she believed me.

"Nora, I love you. You know that. I've been telling you for months. Let me help you."

"How can you help me?"

"You can hide in my place, then see a doctor."

"No doctors. They make reports to the cops."

My patience was wearing thin with her stubborn refusal to seek help. I snapped. "There's one thing for sure – you can't go to work with a fat lip and two black eyes."

A thin chuckle escaped her swollen lip. "Fat chance."

"Then stay at my place, at least until your face heals."

"No questions?"

"No questions. Promise."

~ ~ ~

Thus began the strangest three months of my life. Though my family had money, I had little of my own and they had helped me enough when I was an undergraduate. Living space in the city was at a premium and I'd counted myself lucky to find the efficiency apartment. It had a sofa that made a bed, one easy chair, a kitchen unit set in a closet and a standing room only bath.

During that time I don't believe Nora left my tiny hovel unless she was huddled close to my side. She refused to let me go to her apartment to get her clothes. For a couple of days she made do with an old football jersey of mine. I located a thrift store selling used clothing after I got her a pair of Yogie Bear sneakers at the corner drugstore to replace my ski socks.

She chose jeans and sweaters, a large brim gardening hat, and a multilayered wool poncho that looked like it was made of two squares of fabric with a hole in the middle, but she wouldn't replace the stupid kid's sneakers.

After she exposed the limits of her culinary skills by blowing up the little gas range, we existed on take-out that I would get on my way home from work. Her favorite was Chinese with all the little boxes of samples that could be stretched to last two days.

About two weeks after she moved in, Nora shook me in the middle of the night complaining she was cold. I took her in my arms to share body heat and our relationship changed. Nora was no stranger to the age-old male and female sexual arts. Each movement was cool and precise until she lost herself in the ecstasy of self-fulfillment, then we became groping teenagers discovering new delights in each other.

I'd made her a promise of no questions, but I couldn't help tracing a fading bruise on her cheek and knowing how she'd earned her way before we met. She acknowledged my suspicions with a crooked smile.

Time ran out for our private slice of heaven. My research was finished, my article was submitted for publication, and the lease on the apartment was close to expiring. With help from one of the members of the museum's Board of Trustees I'd managed to secure a teaching position at a small college in Montana.

Nora wasn't happy when I told her about the changes that were taking place in my life. After much pleading on my part, she agreed to marry me and leave the city for the wilds of the far West.

Nora had never ridden on a train and didn't understand my fascination with them. To her, if one had to travel long distances, they flew – which, she admitted, she had never experienced. Her short life had been lived in the city with buses and cars.

I carefully laid my plans to fit my slender pockets. I made reservations on a small feeder line to Minnesota to visit my family where we would be married.

She clung tighter and tighter to the apartment. She was reluctant to meet my family, who, without fail sent care packages of cookies, sausages, and cheese, as if I was stranded in Outer Siberia without proper supplies. It was beyond her to imagine that people still made these things at home in their own kitchens.

In a stumbling way she explained that she felt that she'd be an outsider staring into the window at a family gathering that had 'no admittance' signs posted on every door.

I calmed her fears as best I could – my family is difficult to explain to anyone who has never experienced the multifariousness of generations of diversified nations both Native American and European that have inhabited the northern shores of the Great Lakes.

After the ceremony we'd go to St. Paul to finish our honeymoon journey across the Great Plains to Montana, on the Empire Builder of the Great Northern Railway.

Packing took little time or space. My books and typewriter were boxed and shipped home. We found a small suitcase for her few clothes and walked out of our old lives.

~ ~ ~

We sat on the bench outside the station house, which was closed. The train was delayed and the station master had gone home, as two passengers waiting to board were not something he could be concerned about when supper awaited.

The night was long and cold as we snuggled together to keep warm. We sipped the last of a burnt brew that had sat all day long on a burner. Giving it to us was better than throwing it out – it reminded us of the afternoons spent in the bistro where the coffee was drinkable.

We listened to the whistle of the train off in the distance as it ripped through the gathering fog. The moisture began to settle on our coats. When we stood, Nora's foot slipped on a thin coating of ice starting to coat the platform outside the sheltering roof. I caught her to me and held her away from the seeping cold.

The thundering rumble of the vibrating diesel engines shook the station walls and made the tracks sing with a humming sound like the strings of a harp pulled to capacity. Nora shivered against me, not from cold but fear of the unknown.

I took her hand and placed it on the rail to feel the movement of the train before it came into view. She yanked her hand back as if stung. My lovely Nora had never known the joy of laying her ear on a track to listen to its song. I felt the vibrations ease as the engineer applied the air brakes to slow down the steel monster to pick us up to begin our journey.

There was no pleasant conductor to welcome us aboard and wish us a good journey. The passenger car was hooked to the end of a long row of cattle cars on their way to the slaughterhouses of Chicago, almost as an afterthought, with no caboose. That had gone the way of progress as planes carried the mail now.

There were no steps up into the disreputable Pullman car that must have been resurrected from a long-lost scrap pile.

I lifted Nora up into the doorway, handed her our suitcases, and pulled myself up.

We walked down the corridor peeking into compartments until we find one empty. The engine pulled away from the station before we got our bags stowed under the seats. The jerks threw us both to the floor and we had to scramble up to our seats.

The former elegance of our accommodations had been turned by time and neglect into a cube of dirt and decay. The most that could be said of it was that the compartment was warmer than standing in the wind at the station. The seats and pull down bunk had not been turned into beds in many a year. I hated to think what insects had found a home in the crevices of the rolling junkyard.

We made Nora a little bed on the bench that had the fewest rips with our coats and a few sweatshirts. I used a T-shirt to clean the window on my side to watch the night scenery.

At first Nora gave little jerks each time the whistle blew as the tracks crossed the many country roads over which we traveled. Finally she settled peacefully into sleep as her mind cataloged the sound like it does when sirens blare in city streets in the night.

Crossing lights glowed bright red and the gates were down, blocking invisible traffic when we passed. The roads leading up to the crossings had cracked pavement with weeds growing in the fissures as if few traveled the little lanes. The fencing beside the tracks was sagging on crooked, rotten posts as if no one cared for these dark fields.

A dense fog settled around us. The crossing lights illuminated the dark, dirty smoke-grey mist freezing on trees and fences. The partial moon cast a faint light when the rolling clouds parted for an instant. Little cracks near the edge of the floor allowed sharp drafts of wind to enter the compartment. I tried to pull a piece of loose carpet over them but had to settle for propping my feet on the edge of Nora's berth.

The constant thump, thump, thump of a wheel bearing, badly in need of greasing, lulled me to sleep. I don't know how long I slept before the crashing, grinding sounds of torn metal yanked me to full awareness.

The side of the Pullman was twisted and ripped clear of the rivets that once held it in place. I was pinned to the seat by rusted rails still connected to their ties.

Nora was gone!

The seat where she slept was torn from the floor, half-in and half-out of the car, tilted on its side as if she'd been dumped out into midair.

I screamed her name as I pushed and shoved to get the bent rails off me. I don't know how long I struggled until the rusted pile of twisted steel moved enough for me to slide out through the ripped side of the Pullman, into a nightmare the likes of which has never been seen in Hell.

Cattle were screaming and bawling, climbing over carcasses of the dead to get free from the carnage of their shattered pens. The water of the stream ran red with their blood as it rushed around the scattered cars.

I don't remember how I reached the ground to stumble beside the broken, torn and twisted cars of the train searching for Nora. I called her name, over and over.

Great clouds of steam rose in the frosted air from the engine as it was dragged back down from the far side of the bridge by the weight of the broken cattle cars to its destruction.

The bridge's short span of iron girders and steel cables hung like twisted grapevines and creaked in the wind above my head. I stopped the few men able to move, but they were in a daze and ignored my frantic pleas.

I watched in horror as greyish scavengers rose from around the cattle cars to rush to the Pullman, still balanced precariously above my head. Its side was rolled back like the lid of a can of sardines.

The weight of the Pullman shifted on the twisted rails and rotten ties like the grotesque cartoon of a carriage of death. A man climbed out on the bent platform only to lose his grip as the car plunged to the gorge. His scream echoed in the night.

A deadly silence followed, broken only by sharp sizzles from the engine where it cooled in the stream. My panic increased as I could hear no human sounds.

Where was Nora?

The hooded scavengers were pulling bodies from the wreckage of the Pullman. They stripped them of their clothes and belongings, flinging the naked bodies into the rushing water like discarded refuse. I had to find Nora before those foul subhumans could spoil her beauty.

I searched one side of the wreckage, struggled up the bank to the other side and worked my way down through the brush to the wreck. I spotted the Yogi Bear tennis shoes streaked with mud. Her broken body lay wedged against a concrete pier in a tangle of brush, the bright blue sweater soaked with blood. Her head was bent at a strange angle.

Nora was dead!

Her spirit was lost and frozen like the frost coating the lashes of her staring blue eyes. I pulled her to me and held her, hidden from the scavengers stripping the dead of their final dignity.

A train died the night the bridge collapsed, when I followed my lovely Nora from the darkness into the light of death.

# VANISHING CORPSES

The dark of the moon made the night deeper than usual.

A dense fog formed on No Name Creek. The grey mist swallowed roads and the bridge that spanned the creek. It engulfed the woods on both sides of the stream, then spilled over into the fields and town. It wasn't long until the town of Lynwood could no longer be seen.

An old Ford, traveling too fast for the conditions, crashed onto the bridge over No Name Creek while trying to negotiate the sharp left hand turn on the bridge.

Screams were heard in the night air. A fireball was seen through the fog, as the car exploded into flames.

At the same time of the crash, a scream was heard from the apartment above the grocery store. It was blood-chilling, that final sound of Mrs. Merkle, who'd owned the grocery store and lived in the upstairs apartment. She, too, died that night.

The grocery store had been left to her son, but she was granted a lifetime interest in the property, according to the terms of her late husband's will.

When she became too feeble to work in the store, Bill, their son, assumed the family operation. He worried, but allowed her to remain in the apartment, as it had been her home for twenty years since his father passed away.

When neighbors frantically called him, he rushed to the apartment, but it was too late. She lay on the floor by the window.

Her face was twisted, as if her final agony was engraved there forever. Bill thought his mother had heard the crash or seen the fire and the shock caused her death. The autopsy showed a massive coronary. It was assumed by the coroner she was dead before her body hit the floor. Bill planned to have her cremated and the ashes buried at the foot of his father's grave.

When the mortician came for the body to it take to the crematory, her body was gone!

~ ~ ~

A local farmer trapped muskrats and beaver in No Name Creek to supplement his farm income. The next morning, he waited for the fog to lift before he started out to check his traps. It had been cold enough during the night to freeze the frost on the surface of the bridge it making slippery. When the farmer came upon the wreck on the bridge, he discovered the torched remains of a body twisted around the steel frame under the bridge. A mummified claw, that was once a hand, lay on the bank of the creek.

There was a glittery jelly-like substance floating on the still waters of the creek. To report his discovery, the farmer walked into town following glittering footprints, almost like stardust, on the road.

"Sheriff, while running my traps this morning along No Name Creek, I passed under the bridge where that car crashed last night. Your boys didn't finish cleaning it up. There's a body hanging in the girders above the creek. What looks like a hand almost sprung a trap."

"That's impossible. The driver was in the car. The doors were locked."

"Don't know about that. I'm just telling you what I just seen, not a half hour ago."

Sheriff Buckman knew how indignant old farmers could be when someone disputed their word. "Mr. Benson, describe what you found for me."

"It's in those steel beams under the bridge, all twisted around 'em. Wouldn't have seen it, except some gawker drove across the bridge trying to see something and I looked up. It's kind of hard to tell what it is, looks like one of the Egyptian things I saw once on TV. But that sure is a hand lying by my trap. Go out there and see for yourself."

The Sheriff took him back to the bridge in his patrol car to find the body under the bridge. The sight that greeted him caused him to blink his eyes, scratch his head and stare.

The old Ford was sitting on the bridge, jammed against the railing, as it had been the previous night. Impossible. He'd helped Clyde Thornton pry the burned-out wreckage away from the superstructure of the bridge so he could haul it into town.

He'd stood right there when Clyde cut open the door so the guys from the morgue could remove the charred remains of the driver. He could see that gruesome skull with it's jaw hanging open in a final scream.

Shaken to the core, he wanted to pitch his breakfast, but he knew his job. He put flares in the road to close it from traffic. The sun was slowly burning off the fog, but it wasn't making it any easier to investigate what happened.

Reaching for his radio, he yelled to make himself heard over the dark rushing water. Damn, Mr. Benson had told him when he discovered the second body he'd said the creek was still.

What in the hell was happening? He didn't know, a fact that was making his temper flare. "Deputy, this is the Sheriff. You and the two deputies get out here to No Name Bridge. I need help investigating last night's traffic accident."

Mr. Benson looked at the twisted metal of the old bridge thinking to himself the bridge would have to be replaced. The car was almost unrecognizable.

"Clyde. This is the Sheriff Buckman. I'm here at the bridge at No Name Creek. Bring your wrecker and tools to remove a car that crashed on the bridge. Take the debris to your junkyard and put it in the county's inbound area under lock and key."

"Sheriff, I did that last night. In fact I haven't dropped it."

"Go look. If I'm not a monkey's uncle, it's back out here."

"That's impossible."

"Said the same, but I know what I'm looking at this very minute. Get the hell out here."

"On my way." The phone slammed down in his ear as the farmer tapped on his shoulder.

"Got to get back, this running to town has put me behind feeding."

Mr. Benson led Sheriff Buckman down the treacherous cliff path below the bridge and pointed to his discoveries.

The old man had told him the truth. A second body was welded to the piers of the bridge.

~ ~ ~

Later, as the wrecker dragged the twisted remains of the wreckage through town several people saw old Mrs. Merkle standing at her bedroom window. By that time, most knew she had died during the night.

A couple of weeks after the accident, the Sheriff was out on patrol. About 10:00 pm, out of the corner of his eye, he saw what he knew to be an old lady floating down Main Street. He swore the cloudy image was the torso of Mrs. Merkle. He didn't mention it in his patrol report for fear someone would think he'd been drinking or had lost his mind.

Bill Merkle didn't say anything about the disappearance of his mother's body. He buried an empty box in End of the Road Cemetery to keep down rumors. His act was futile as the coroner had gotten drunk one night and told his buddies about the missing corpse. Sheriff Buckman had heard the strange tale, which did nothing to explain what he'd seen in the night.

Later that week, one of the deputies was on patrol and noticed movement in the grocery as he drove past. He stopped in the next block and walked back to the store. He tried the front and back doors, both were locked. He shined his light in the windows to investigate the best he could. He saw a cloudy image moving things from shelf to shelf. Like the Sheriff, he didn't mention anything in his report. He did ask the Sheriff if he had seen anything odd the last time he went on patrol.

"No, nothing out of the ordinary. Why? Did you see something unusual?"

"I thought I saw something in Merkle's Grocery on Main Street. But it was nothing."

Autopsy reports on the victims in the car crash trickled into the coroner's office. A high level of alcohol and cocaine was found in the blood of the driver. The coroner got on the phone to report the findings.

"Sheriff, this is Dr. Stone. The autopsy reports are finished and on my desk. Could you meet me at the junkyard about noon tomorrow?"

"I'll be there, Doc."

"You'll need copies. I'll bring them with me."

The Sheriff closed his file on the accident and death of the driver as due to driving too fast for the road conditions, while intoxicated from an overdose of alcohol and cocaine.

His next call was from Clyde Warren, the owner of the wrecker service.

"I was planning to crush the car from the bridge crash this morning, but it's gone again."

"What? Doc Stone wants me to meet him out there tomorrow. He has something on his mind."

The Sheriff and Clyde searched the junkyard, but they found nothing. There wasn't even any evidence of anybody dragging a car off. The Sheriff drove every street in town and the surrounding country until dark, but again, found nothing. He and his deputies kept their eyes peeled for weeks while on patrol, checking overgrown logging lanes, abandoned houses and decaying barns. Their search never turned up one clue. As time passed, the futile search ended.

The Sheriff's office occasionally got calls that the old lady from the store was seen roaming the streets at night.

He passed it off as people imaging things, refusing to admit to the dispatcher what he'd seen with his own eyes.

While working late one evening, he got the feeling someone was watching him. Looking up from his desk, he didn't see anything, but the creepy sensation persisted and he couldn't concentrate on his work. He went out the back door to the alley behind the office and around the building. There was nothing. He came to the front of his office, checked both directions on Main Street. The hour was late; nothing moved on the empty street.

Then he saw them. Footprints glowed on the sidewalk below the window of his office. He got his camera to get a picture of the strange sight. The light meter in the camera indicated there was just enough light, filtering through a light fog that was settling over the valley to get an exposure. The Sheriff followed the footprints until they stopped beside the grocery store that Mrs. Merkle owned and worked, before she died in the apartment above it.

Every story, every rumor he'd ever heard about the place flashed through his mind. If anyone had been listening they would have heard him mutter to himself, "No! It can't be."

From the angle where he was standing he could see a faint light in the back of the drugstore. The druggist was working late. He developed film himself on a rush order, instead of sending it off.

The Sheriff crossed the street and knocked on the door loud enough for the old man to hear him. He begged him to put a rush on his film and hurried back to the jail to lock up. He'd had enough weird stuff for the night.

The next morning at the café the old druggist handed him a thick yellow envelope.

"Sheriff, here's your pictures."

"Let's see how they came out."

"There's nothing on the film."

"What do you mean? There has to be something."

"While the prints were in the solution I saw a face. When I took 'em out of the dryer they were blacker than a witch's titty. What were you trying to take a picture of?"

"Footprints. There were footprints on the sidewalk below my office window. They led up the street to the ally beside the grocery store, then stopped."

"Beats me – nothing like that is on the film or the prints."

~ ~ ~

"Sheriff, this is Clyde from the junkyard."

"What can I do for you?"

"You know that car we hauled in from that wrecked on the bridge over No Name creek? One that disappeared?"

"Yeah. What about it?"

"Well…it's back."

109

"What do you mean it's back? A pile of twisted steel can't just reappear."

"While making my rounds last night, like I always do. There was a spot on the ground where it had sat – it was glowing a bright green. Figured it was something that dripped off the car after the fire. It was still pretty hot the first time I drug her in. Weird thing, that car coming-and-going whenever it takes a notion, like the Blue Tick hound of mine. Looked to me like melted paint or runny axle grease."

When Clyde got wound up and a-going he could talk your arm off and never get to the point. The Sheriff had to stop him before he worked up a full head of steam. "So. You said the car was back."

"What I called you about! This morning that dad-blame car is sitting out there at the back of the lot. Pretty as you please.

"Found a snag on the fence. Looks like a piece of a fleece lined leather jacket."

The Sheriff thought a minute. He hated to invite Clyde to the office – he'd never get rid of him. But the car, back on the lot, was strange. Worse than that, it was downright bizarre. He'd walked that lot himself when it disappeared. He knew it wasn't there.

"Bring it over. Leave it out front with my deputy. I've got to run out to Four Corners. I'll send it to the state lab, maybe they can tell us where it came from."

He pressed the plunger down on the phone, cutting Clyde off, but kept on talking on the disconnected line – to himself.

"Maybe they can provide me with a clue about an accident where two men burned to death. One outside a locked car. A wrecked old Ford that comes and goes over a chain-link fence, topped with barbed wire. Footprints that glow, but don't photograph, all before they haul me off to the funny farm."

~ ~ ~

A call came in from the State lab.

"Sheriff, I have the lab report on that piece of leather you sent me. It's a piece of sheepskin leather with the fleece on it. More than likely from a coat. A home-tanned skin, still had traces of Fels Napa on the skin side. Very fine piece of work, soft like kid's skin. Don't see much of that quality around anymore, most sheepskin coats are stiff as a board."

"Old Man Harvey is the only one in these parts that raises sheep."

"Does he make things with his own hides?"

"I'll drive out to his place and ask. Seems like he does do special order work. Too expensive for anyone around here. See if he remembers anything about a coat like you describe. It's not far."

When the Sheriff arrived, Mr. Harvey was not in sight.

The front door was open and a still warm coffee cup was on a table by an easy chair.

"Harvey, are you in here? It's Sheriff Buckman. I want to talk to you."

"Come on back. I'm working in the lean-to."

"What are you doing, Harvey?"

"Oh, I'm getting ready to lay out a pattern for a poncho. A customer wants me to make him one before it gets really cold. Easy to lift his rifle when he goes deer hunting."

"Where does he live?"

"Up near the end of Wilbur Hollow, on a branch of No Name Creek."

"Have you ever made anything like a jacket or coat?"

"This past spring a fellow over in Briar Patch ordered a knee length coat. Paid cash for it when he picked it up."

"Did you by any chance get a name or address?"

"Nope. I do a cash business. I don't ask for names and addresses. When someone orders something I tell them when it will be ready and they come pick it up. Don't make enough to fool with Infernal Revenue. Why?"

"A piece of a sheepskin coat was found at the junkyard near the spot where I was keeping the car that wrecked on the bridge over No Name Creek."

"Could be mine. I don't know. Have to see it."

"It's over at the State Police Lab. Sorry to have bothered you."

"That's alright. Any time. Wish I could have been more help Sheriff. Come again, anytime."

The Sheriff was sitting in his office, mumbling to himself about the footprints on the sidewalk that he found in front of the office, when he returned from Harvey's sheep ranch. Were they the same fluorescent green that led to town from the wreck on the bridge at No Name creek? The farmer who reported the wreck said he followed glowing footprints to town.

Hearing him one of his deputies stuck his head in the door. "What did you say, Sheriff?"

"Nothing, Mike. Just talking to myself."

"That's okay as long as you don't answer yourself. Did you solve anything while you were out to old Man Harvey's?"

"No."

~ ~ ~

From time to time the Sheriff would get calls that the gray smokey image of the old lady was seen in and around the stores at night. Merchandise was found missing or rearranged on the store's shelves. In the morning, after one of these sightings, Bill Merkle put boxes of cereal boxes back where they belonged. His soap powder had been removed from the shelves and was stacked on the floor. It wasn't long until money Bill hadn't deposited in the bank at the end of the day started coming up missing.

A year later a man came into the store.

"Hi. My name is Sam Farmer. I understand you might have an apartment to rent? I would like to rent it, if it's still available. I need a place to stay till I get back on my feet."

Bill looked the middle-aged man over; hair was cut, clothes were clean, and face shaved. No wandering hippie cadging a handout while searching for enlightenment. To him, the man was a godsend. With someone living upstairs maybe folks would stop talking about seeing things. He and his wife hadn't had a moment's peace since his mother died.

"Pleased to meet you. I'm Bill Merkle. The apartment is available. There is a job opening in the store. You can work off the rent if you're short of cash."

"When can I start?"

"In the morning, see you about nine o'clock. Follow me. I'll show you the way to the apartment. Here's the key."

Sam was a complete stranger. Nobody knew anything about him or where he came from. He was such an ordinary person, no one thought to ask questions. He just showed up that morning, looking for a place to stay and a job.

He agreed to clean after closing and do other light chores to help pay his rent. It wasn't long after he moved in that he was spending more and more time working in the store during the day. He started waiting on customers, which gave Bill a day off to take his wife on a short trip. He ate most of his meals in the small café on the corner, and while he wasn't a gossipy sort, he was always pleasant to whoever was sitting next to him. Being willing to share his morning paper went a long way to establishing himself in the community.

Eventually, Sam Farmer became a member of the church and the local Lions Club. He wasn't stingy with his free time and worked on projects as well as pitching in where needed about town. It was obvious he loved kids and enjoyed their company. He told the minister the young children kept him feeling young.

~ ~ ~

Bill Merkle called, "Sheriff, could we meet later today?"

"Stop in anytime. I'll be in the office all day."

It took Bill Merkle all day to work up the gumption to go see Sheriff Buckman. He didn't have a thing, except a funny feeling, that something wasn't right about Sam Farmer. It was almost closing time when he took off his apron, grabbed his jacket and left the grocery.

"What did you need to see me about, Bill?"

"I'm curious about Sam Farmer. He has moved in too fast for me. Could you investigate him without being too obvious?"

"Why?"

"I don't trust him."

"Did Sam ever say where he's from?"

"Never mentioned it. Come to think about it, he's never said anything about where he came from, family or friends. It's like his life started the day he walked into the store, wanting to rent Mom's apartment. I hadn't advertised it or anything, but he knew it was empty."

"I can't very well investigate someone without having a place to start. How long has Sam worked for you?"

"Little over a year."

"He's been working for you more than a year and all of a sudden you don't trust him. It took you long enough to work up a dislike for the guy. What has he done?"

"Nothing. It's just a feeling I've gotten lately. You know, when someone is too accommodating."

"You get me a name of a place. In the meantime I'll ask around."

"I could go through his things."

"No. I'll look into it. Will let you know if anyone has turned up missing. Maybe he stopped someplace else looking for work. Not many strangers come through that someone wouldn't remember."

"I best be going."

"Bill, better yet, if you can get me a glass or something he's handled. If he was in the military his fingerprints will be on file."

Sheriff Buckman walked Bill to the door. While they had been talking, a dense fog was settling in to engulf the town.

It was coming from the direction of the bridge over No Name Creek.

"Would you look at that. Radio didn't mention fog rolling in tonight."

"Whee! What's that awful odor?"

"It smells like something dead. Wonder if the farmers have been dumping waste in the creek. They'll do it every time my back is turned."

"I had best get back to the store before this fog gets worse."

The fingerprints on a glass Bill obtained, by having Sam help him rearranged a shelf of glasses, alerted the Sheriff as to the true identity of Sam Farmer. He came from Texas where he had been in prison for armed robbery and assault until he escaped. He was a wanted man and considered very dangerous. His real name was Roy Bell Conners.

The last thing Sheriff Buckman wanted was to tell Bill Merkle the truth. Bill was capable of doing something stupid.

"Bill, this is the Sheriff. Do you have a couple of cases of 30 weight oil in stock?"

"Give me a minute, I'll check."

The Sheriff drummed his fingers on his desk while he waited for Bill to return to the phone. He knew he wasn't as fast as he was in his younger days. An escaped con like Roy Conners would be packing. Still, he knew how to get the drop on a mean drunk out at Four Corners' Roadhouse, though they did run more to knives than guns. He didn't want to get anyone hurt by botching his job, least of all Bill or himself for that matter.

"Sheriff?"

"I'm still here."

"That's what I've got in the back room. Two unopened cases."

"Bill, is your man Sam around?"

"Yes, he's here."

"Would he be willing to help me load them in the patrol car? My lumbago is acting up."

The Sheriff could hear Bill asking as he made his plans for what he knew was the most dangerous arrest he'd ever made.

"He says sure, he'd be glad to."

"That storeroom has a back door. I'll pull in the alley beside it. That'll save you lugging those heavy cases out front."

"Thanks."

"I'll be right over."

When Sheriff Buckman pulled up, the man known as Sam Farmer was standing in the alley holding a case of oil. Bill Merkle was in the open doorway holding the second case. The Sheriff wasn't pleased to see Bill. Why couldn't a customer be in the grocery to keep Bill busy and out of his way? No help for it now.

The Sheriff got out, walked around to the trunk and popped the lock. He asked Bill about his kid, who played baseball on the high school team to get his attention away from the con.

He walked around the cruiser, opening the deck lid with his left hand, then moved to the side to give the man room to load the case and, out of sight, opened the back door of the car with his right, still asking questions about Bill's family.

Roy Conners did just as he expected. He carried the case to the open trunk, bent and placed it on the mat. When he was pulling back to straighten up, his arms were bent at a 45 degree angle. Sheriff Buckman shoved a piece of lead water pipe between his elbows and back. Snapped a handcuff on his right wrist, worked the cuffs under Conners' belt, then pulled his left wrist back for the second cuff.

He yanked up Conner's shirt and extracted a 45 Army Colt that was in danger of slipping down into his pants as his belt was doing extra duty and laid it on the case of oil.

He spun Conners around the car by the pipe and shoved him into the back seat, slamming the door to lock him in tight. Sheriff Buckman was nothing but bull strong. He hadn't given Conners time to react before he had him hogtied. His old bar trick worked with no one hurt.

Bill Merkle was still holding the case of oil with his mouth hanging open. He never knew the old sheriff could move so fast.

"Come on, Bill. Put that case in the trunk. I haven't got all day. That oil came in right handy. We'll use it one day."

"Yes, Sir."

The Sheriff felt sorry for Bill as he emptied the gun Conners had concealed under his shirt.

"Your man Sam is on the run from the law. He escaped from prison in Texas awhile back. His real name is Roy Bell Conners. I'll arrest him tonight for holding and file charges against him in the morning."

After booking and locking Conners in jail, the Sheriff contacted the Texas State Police.

"This is Sheriff Buckman in Lynwood, Kentucky."

"What can we do for you, Sheriff?"

"I arrested your man, Roy Bell Conners on suspicion tonight."

"What did he do?"

"That's the problem…nothing. He's worked at the local grocery for about a year. Lived as a model citizen under the name of Sam Farmer."

"You can hold him on our outstanding warrant. We'll be up to get him as soon as possible."

~ ~ ~

"Conners. Here's your breakfast."

The Sheriff stared at the cell dumb-founded. He'd locked Conners in last night to hold him for the Texas State Police.

The cell was empty! Roy Conners was gone.

How in the hell had he managed an escape? This cell was still locked. The Sheriff had all the keys in his pocket. He wasn't fool enough to leave the key in the office overnight. He'd carried them for twenty years. His wife was always complaining about having to replace the pockets of his pants before they wore out. She said he clanked when he walked.

No bars were bent. The cell had no windows.

How in the Sam Hill had he gotten out of that cell? Yet the man had escaped.

He raced into his office to call Bill Merkle.

"This is the Sheriff, are you at the store?"

"No, I picked up here at the house. I was getting ready to leave. What's wrong?"

"Sam Farmer…Roy Conners has escaped."

"How?"

"I don't know. He's just vanished. Meet me at the store with keys to your mother's apartment."

"Okay."

Bill was unlocking the front door as the sheriff ran up the street. Both of them failed to see the bank of fog rolling up from the creek.

"Sam had a set of keys."

"I just checked. They're locked in the office safe with that gun I took off him. They're still there. I opened it after I called you. Be careful, let me go in first."

"How do you get up to the apartment?"

"Stairs in the storeroom. Here's the key."

When the Sheriff opened the door to Bill's mother's apartment – they stared in shock. It was empty.

Dust covered everything. Spider webs hung like curtains from the ceiling and across the windows around the rooms. There were no human footprints in the dust, just little scratches of mouse scurries and a trail of rice-sized turds. No living soul had been in the apartment in months, maybe over a year.

Where had Roy Conners, alias Sam Farmer, lived all those months, when he was pretending to rent the apartment?

"But someone…was here."

"How do you know?"

"Downstairs. All of the bags of jerky are gone from the racks."

They returned to the front of the store. The windows were grey and rivulets of moisture ran down them.

"Any signs of a break-in?"

"None. The doors were locked when we came in. I checked the back door, before I followed you up the stairs, because I saw the missing bags."

"I'm going to do a walking patrol when the fog lifts. He can't have gone far in this thick soup."

Some of the buildings on the far edge of town were

covered with black slime. When the Sheriff touched it, it was slick and cold like a wet plastic garbage sack. At the edge of town, near the junkyard, two of the town's storage buildings had been reduced to a pile of ashes.

Sheriff Buckman could smell the residue of the wet ashes, but he was scratching his chin. No one had reported a fire during the night, not even the Widow Fairfield (who called him if a chipmunk ran across her porch during the night).

The muffled sounds of screams, coming from the park by the creek, sent him running across the road and down the hill. He could see flames leaping from the storage shed.

The door stood open. Smoke poured out in billowing rolls, but no flames. Faint groans of pain sent the Sheriff to his knees, to crawled under the smoke. Someone was in there and needed help.

Inside the building he stood up. It was clear, no smoke, no sign of a fire. The Sheriff found two bodies burned beyond recognition. There was no question – they were dead.

Outside, the roof of the shed smoldered, like a dying campfire. The Sheriff called 911.

"Send an EMS unit to the park."

"Who is this?"

"Sheriff Buckman. There are two charred bodies in the park tool shed."

"We're on our way."

A fire truck came with the medical unit. They doused the roof with water and then the bodies were removed and taken to the morgue.

"Sheriff, how come those bodies were burned so badly, that you can't recognize them, but the fire was minor like maybe a Roman candle hit the roof?"

"I don't know. Need to call the state arson team."

Later that afternoon two men arrived, who looked over the little building.

"Sheriff, all we found is a black slime on the structure. Why did you call us for something so trivial?"

He explained about the bodies found inside, that were burned so badly they were twisted and bent out of shape. The men requested a visit to the morgue.

It was the last place the Sheriff wanted to visit. He seen enough burn victims when they had to pry, what remained of that fellow a year ago, off the bridge trusses. What was left of his skin came off in strips like a barbecued pig. The Sheriff would never forget the claw of a hand lying beside Mr. Benson's trap. Then there was the driver of the old Ford. Cooked until what was left of human bones were so fragile they almost crumbled when touched.

At the morgue, one guy ran for the toilet. The other gritted his teeth so hard he bit his lip. Both of them, seasoned veterans, couldn't get out of the morgue fast enough.

"Our report will state the cause is of a suspicious nature. An act of God…maybe lightening."

The arson team left, still a little green around the gills, before the sheriff's phone rang.

"Sheriff. Stone here. I'm calling from the emergency room."

"What can I do for you, Doc?"

"We've had nine people come in this morning with third degree burns over 50% of their bodies! Thought you would like to know."

"Are they still alive?"

"Just. Doing everything we can to save them, but we're not equipped to handle burns of this magnitude."

"Did they have any identification on them?"

"No. If they die we'll try to identify them through dental records."

"Who brought them in?"

"Don't know."

"What do you mean? You 'don't know.'"

"That's just it. A nurse found them outside the doors this morning, stacked like cord wood."

"What?"

"Got to go. Problems."

"Let me know…" The Sheriff replaced the receiver. He was talking to a dead line.

While filling out reports on what he found in the park, the Sheriff's desk began to vibrate. Then near quitting time his coat rack, holding his jacket and gun belt, fell to the floor. Little shakes from the fault near the river were nothing new.

He set the coat rack to rights and went back to work, pecking the words out on his old Royal. All at once the coat rack moved slowly across the floor and down the hall, like it was being pulled with a string. It stopped in front of the empty cells.

The sheriff was rubbing his eyes and shaking. The coat rack had stopped in front of the cell Roy Conners escaped from during the night. Were all the strange fires a ruse to keep him busy so Conners could have time to make a clean getaway?

He'd had enough and was getting close to losing his temper.

The phone rang. Muttering, "What now?"

"Sheriff Buckman?"

"Yes."

"I am, Captain L.B. Reynolds of the Texas State Police. You called us yesterday about arresting a man, by the name of Roy Bell Conners."

"Yes, but he escaped during the night. My deputy is out looking for him this very minute."

"We're sorry, Sir. You had the wrong man. Roy Bell Conners died in an automobile wreck up your way, over a year ago. He was driving an old Ford."

"That's impossible! I got his name from an Army fingerprint file and the police phonographs matched the man I arrested."

"Sir, I'm reading the autopsy lab report from the Kentucky Crime Lab, as we speak. The body was identified from dental records of fillings done at the prison. I don't know why you weren't informed, as he died in your jurisdiction."

"I see."

"Funny thing. His mother requested the remains be shipped back here for burial in a family plot. When the casket arrived, it was empty. That's why we never closed the file."

"Thank you. Captain. Would it be too much trouble for you to mail me a copy of that report for my files?"

"Be pleased to, Sheriff. If you don't mind me saying so, if Sam Farmer was Roy Bell Conners, he's the only man I ever heard of who escaped death by burning in hell first."

~ ~ ~

"Sheriff. This is Dr. Stone. Sorry to take so long to get back to you.

"All of the burn victims died. They showed no improvement. They didn't last a week. We had them on life support, but it didn't help. My autopsy didn't tell us anything we didn't already know. There were three men,

127

two women, and four children. I'd say the kids were between seven and nine. Two might have been twins. They died from their burns. Don't think they were from around here. If they were, they never went to a local dentist."

"Thanks for letting me know."

"We need to cremate them soon. We've had them a week. They're starting to decay rapidly. But we need your okay before we can proceed."

"Can you hold 'em for a couple more days? I'll send a state-wide notice. Maybe someone will have a missing person report. If I don't hear anything in a week we'll close the file."

"While we're on the subject there are two more burned bodies in the morgue that were pulled out of the shed at the park. Could you do an autopsy on them?"

"Got curious. Saw them. Can tell you now, my best guess is they are a middle-aged man and an old woman."

"Thanks. I'll drop by your office and pick up the reports."

Three weeks later fog engulfed the town again.

"Sheriff, this is Clyde."

"What can I do for you?"

"You had best get over here as soon as you can."

"What's wrong?"

"You'll see when you get here."

Clyde was standing by the gate, waiting as if he was afraid to enter his own salvage yard.

128

"When I opened this morning, you see what I found. That old Ford has melted down like it came out of a foundry furnace. Don't get too close. That pile is still hot."

The smoke rising off of it look like the steam coming from his wife's teakettle when the water was boiling.

"How'd this happen?"

"Sheriff, I don't know. There was heavy dense fog this morning."

"Know that, Clyde."

"Two of my buildings burn a month ago for no reason. They were covered with black slime like this Ford. Then the tool shed in the park smokes, but doesn't burn. All happens when we get a bad fog."

"Something evil about that fog, like you read in the Bible when folks have been sinning. It rolls in, out of nowhere, thick as pea soup, and something or someone burns."

The sheriff turned away and headed back to his office. When Clyde's rambling started to make sense, it was time to review all the facts.

Smokey images of Mrs. Merkle, who died in her apartment above the store, on the night of the crash on the bridge, over No Name Creek had been seen the night before each fog that engulfed the town.

The thick fog always started at the creek, carrying a rotten odor, then rolled into town, as if it was pushed by a steamroller.

Eleven people had died in a fierce fire that few had seen and smelled. Two more were dead if you counted Mrs. Merkle and Roy Bell Connors. That made thirteen. Mrs. Merkle and Conner's bodies had disappeared before burial and had never been found.

Things were quiet while Sam Farmer worked at the grocery and didn't take up again until the night he was arrested, as Roy Conners. The sheriff remembered the man had never said a word from the time he snapped the cuffs on him.

A burned out old Ford had been sitting in the junkyard. He helped load it on the wrecker himself. It disappeared, then reappeared, and finally ended up a melted lump of steel months later.

Someone was walking around with a hole in an expensive coat made by Old Man Harvey. Where that little piece of evidence fit in the puzzle Sheriff Buckman had no idea.

In the middle of his musings the phone rang.

"Sheriff's Office."

"This is Dr. Stone."

"How can I help?"

"I sent those bodies you found at the park to the State Crime Lab. There was something funny about them."

"What?"

"I told you I figured them for a middle-age man and an old woman. That's what they were, but the burns weren't fresh. Those corpses were mummies that had been dead over a year."

"Doc, are you serious?"

"Very. The woman was Mrs. Merkle. Her rose gold wedding ring was melted into what was left of the finger bone. If you remember it had a pinkish color – she was proud of that ring."

"My God! Bill buried her ashes in End of the Road. I attended the funeral."

"Don't know what he buried, but it wasn't his mother."

"The man?"

"I missed it there. Didn't take a close enough look."

"Remember that heavy belt buckle of a running horse Sam Farmer always wore?"

"Y…es."

"It was lodged against what was left of his backbone. That man was a Roy Bell Conners from Texas. It gets worse."

"How can it?"

"Their bodies have vanished."

Sheriff Buckman hung up the phone and stared down at the thick file on his desk.

Outside a thick fog rolled up against his office window. His head nodded, then his body slumped in his chair, as the file began to burn.

# JOURNEY HOME

The storm came fast and furious.

I'd checked the weather before I started. There was no mention of expected travel problems or I'd have called and canceled. A lifetime of living rough had taught me to survive under adverse conditions, but it was not a state I craved for a holiday.

A fleece-lined flight jacket is on the seat beside me. I'd pulled it from the back of my closet, as a last-minute precaution to take into account for Maine weather close to the sea.

A single, two-lane road winds from Challis to Bangor. The land beside it is lined with endless trees and it constantly curves back and forth on itself. The old rental Jeep is no stranger to my hands as we tool along the winding path in the fading light. According to my sketch of landmarks, rapidly disappearing in the gloom, I'm about fifteen miles from the turnoff to the family holdings when the snow starts.

Herbert Vest is the distant cousin on my father's side, who insisted I come for a visit as it was time I met relatives who'd followed my career. Family is something I have little of and can't say I miss, since I've never seen most of them.

The years have flown faster than I care to admit since I first met Herbert at Aunt Jo's funeral. We'd kept in touch with random postcards that expressed little except weather and health reports. He'd be appalled if a personal note appeared on a card for all to see, as it passed through the mail. Near forty, with a gracious, kindly manner, he believes it's his duty to keep track of wandering relatives, no matter where they may be hanging their hat.

How many years have passed since I'd been in the United States long enough to take a week off to make a journey to the place my dad called home? Like me, his life was lived on foreign soil.

As I drive through the thickening snow I cross my fingers, hoping some ambitious potentate wouldn't start up a war somewhere in the world. My editor would be calling, demanding I fly into the battle with my camera and no one to cover my back. I'd been a fool to leave him Herbert's phone number.

I cannot help remembering the Pulitzer winning photo of a camera, lying in the desert sands, with a hole through the middle of the lens. Would the day come when I'd be the poor bloke who held the camera, intent on getting one last shot? I much prefer living to having any expectation of an award-winning photo – the price those daredevils pay for the spectacular is more than I can afford.

I haven't encountered another vehicle in what seems like hours. Without a radio there isn't much to do while driving through a thick curtain of snow and ice but think and remember.

My father was a groundman stationed in England during the war. Then he followed the digs of his chosen profession of archaeology and anthropology. After my mother died, he packed me with his baggage, to acquire an education, excellent as I later realized, but at the time, was managed in a catch-as-catch-can fashion.

When I'm state-side, I live in the Greenwich Village flat owned by my mother's sister, Josephine Lure. Aunt Jo took me in when my father was killed, in a landslide in Turkey. I bunked with her while studying for a degree in photojournalism, at New York City College.

The degree and the fact I could speak a smattering of a dozen different languages, got me my one and only job with a small upstate paper that prefers to use original material instead of wire services for their overseas coverage.

We meshed. My wanderlust is financed at their expense plus a regular paycheck. I worry that one day they'll be bought out by a big city daily and I'll be out of a job.

I'm curious as to why Herbert wants me to meet some distant relatives so badly he called the newspaper and insisted they make me get in touch with him by phone. Our grandfathers were half-brothers, which is a nebulous connection at best. Why he continues to live in his ancient mausoleum, lost in the backwoods of nowhere is beyond me.

It isn't lack of funds. His great-grandfather made the family money. Even though it has filtered down four generations, it's still more than enough to get by on. I can't remember my dad mentioning any of his family who actually worked for a living as he did.

My grandfather was a riverboat gambler, who, when he was flush, spent it high living. When he was busted, he sponged off a relative. Dad grew up in the family home and acquired some of the frugality traits of his step-great-uncle, who was Herbert's grandfather.

I slow the Jeep to a crawl as the snow, propelled before the wind, makes visibility damn near impossible. I'm literally driving by the seat of my pants, as I've done many times, creeping on trails hacked into the side of rough mountains in the dark to avoid random mortar fire. I whip the steering wheel to avoid a moose blocking the road. The Jeep slides. I fight hard to steer into the skid, but it plunges forward into space.

The cold and the barking of a dog bring me around. No idea how long I've been out. Rub my hand across my face trying to get my bearings – I'll have a whopper of a goose egg on my forehead to meet the relatives. My head had slammed against the steering wheel.

Try to start the Jeep, but the old vehicle isn't having any part of it. I'm not prepared for a trek through the snow. My Italian loafers won't last long. Already, I can feel the intense cold as I struggle to pull my fleece jacket over the Irish fisherman's sweater I'm wearing over a dress shirt.

The dog keeps barking as if to say "stop stalling and get on with it. You're going to have to walk, whether you want to or not."

It can't be far to civilization when a dog is out here in the wind and a storm.

I rummage around in the glove box and find an old flashlight. The batteries are feeble at best. It must be used sparingly, to get me to where I can find help.

The dog seems to know where he's going. I follow him as he races over the deepening snow. Have a difficult time walking. My loafers get stuck in the mess and pull off. At times, the dog will stop, look back and bark, as if telling me to get a move on. He's impatient to find a warm home.

Sharp needles of ice sting my neck below the brim of my heavy leather hat. It's a wet snow mixed with sleet that freezes as soon as it hits. The storm gods are kind as the wind is at my back, pushing me along. I pull the collar of my jacket up around my ears and trudge on, trying to keep my eyes on the dog's paw prints, but they vanish in the blowing snow.

Suddenly, massive stone pillars mark a driveway like the entrance to some baronial fief. A coal oil lantern, flickering with feeble light hangs from a rusted hinge. The dog disappears as I plunge up the long lane. The accumulated snow is past my ankles, soaking my pantlegs. Slushy mush. Cold feet can feel each stone of the gravel drive through the thin soles of my shoes.

Herbert jerks open the door before I can reach for the knocker. "Get in here! We waited supper, but it got late. Where have you been?"

"Ran off the road. Jeep is in a ditch with the back wheels in the air. Need a tow truck to pull it out."

He takes my jacket and tosses it on the carved newel post at the bottom of the stairs. Shakes my hat and sails it in the same direction.

"That must wait till morning when they clear the roads. I'll make a call for the road crew to be on the lookout for it. How did you ever find us walking, in this blizzard?"

"A dog led me to the turnoff and up to the house until I could see your lights."

"Dog! What kind of dog?"

"Border Collie, from what I could see. Strange eyes. They glowed in the dark."

"Oh dear."

137

"What's with the 'oh dear'?"

"Turk has been dead for forty years. When a family member sees him, it means there will be a death in the family."

"My father never told me that story."

"Probably never heard it. It was after he lived here. Morbid really. Forget it. Come, I want you to meet some of your family."

He leads me down a long hall to what may have once been called a drawing room. My loafers make a squishing sound on the stone floor. Today, the long room is used mainly as a library/sitting room. Books line the walls, are stacked on the floor, and are piled on every available flat surface.

Seated on a long sofa, facing a huge fireplace, are four people whose heads swivel to face us as we enter the room – two men and two women of varying ages. Four armchairs sit closer to the fire. Two are occupied by an older man and an elderly woman. A young woman is standing near long French doors, thumbing the pages of a book while staring out into the night. She doesn't bother to glance our way.

Herbert takes my arm and leads me around to stand facing the group on the sofa. I feel like some heathen idol that has been placed on display before a disinterested audience. Not a muscle in their faces moves, it's as if I'm invisible, yet my wet footprints mark our path across the worn carpet.

"Valerie, come over here and meet your cousin."

She turns, not pretty in the accepted sense, but an interesting face. Photogenic with high cheekbones, a broad mouth and dark eyes that are too large for her face.

She starts to take a step toward us when a loud thump sounds behind her. The French doors burst open. A bloody hand falls to the floor, attached to the body of a man.

Bedlam breaks loose. The grey-faced blonde on the sofa screams and faints into the arms of the sporting guy sitting next to her as he tries to rise, sending them both tumbling to the floor.

Herbert mutters, "Oh dear," and collapses into a chair, wiping his forehead as if he is hot.

The couples on the sofa look on, with bored expressions as if they are watching a bad play.

The gentleman in the chair reaches to the floor, picks up a shawl and wraps it around the older woman next to him.

He shouts, "For the love of the almighty, someone shut that damn door! Mother will take a chill."

Valerie kneels beside the body and looks up at me. "It's Delbert. I think he's dead."

I have no idea how I've crossed the room. Reporter instinct, I suspect.

A quick look from the side shows the face of the body that looks surprisingly like Herbert, lying in the open door. There is a double-bladed axe imbedded in the middle of his back.

Valerie reaches out to him.

"No. Don't touch. Let me get my camera. Then I can pull him in and shut the door."

I start to the hall, yelling at Herbert. "Call the police."

I rummage through my duffel, unwrap the Polaroid I'd protected with a pair of shorts, dart back to the library, and kick off the soaked loafers inside the door. My feet are freezing.

Herbert has gotten a grip on himself while I was gone. "Walter, take your mother upstairs and put her to bed."

"But she'll want to know what is happening."

"No, Walter. You want to know. You can see someone has cleaved my bother with the axe."

He waves a limp hand in my direction. "This is your cousin, Gilbert Vest. He is a photographer, who has a job to do. Then we can close the door."

As I shove a fresh film pack in the camera, I give the relatives a brief nod. Valerie stands in one smooth move and steps aside to give me room to work. One very cool cousin.

"Delbert is Herbert's twin. He suffered brain damage at birth. Sweetheart of a guy," she explains.

I look at her while I'm waiting for the first photo to process and silently cock an eyebrow. She doesn't miss a cue.

"Nurse. Bellevue. Trauma unit. Hitch in 'Nam. Isn't much I haven't seen."

She glances over to Herbert, who has his fist stuffed in his mouth to keep from screaming.

"Herbert is…was devoted to him. Let me give him something to do before he collapses."

I nod to her and continue working. I can hear her clear voice behind me, giving orders like an army drill sergeant. She doesn't take any backchat but sends the rest of the crew off to bed like an efficient nanny before dumping punch in an antique skillet and sticking it on the fire to warm.

By the time I finish the last shot of the body and pull it inside to close the door, she has Herbert sipping heavily doused punch from a silver loving cup.

"My dear, this is a trifle dusty."

"Doesn't matter – there is enough brandy in the punch for effective sterilization."

She looks at me. "Can you keep him occupied while I find some mugs in the kitchen? When I get back, I'll help you move Delbert to a safe place, until the police get here."

Herbert speaks up, "Use the billiard table…down the hall, far side. Open a window…it'll stay cool. Police aren't coming."

Valerie and I speak as one. "Police aren't coming?"

"Tried to call. Lines are down. No service." Herbert is starting to come apart at the seams.

"Val." It seems natural to shorten her name. "Let's get Delbert down the hall. You lead the way."

It is awkward struggling to get the body on my shoulder for a fireman's lift and not disturb the axe. With her help I manage and am grateful *rigor mortis* is not a problem.

We stretch him out on the billiard table – face down, pretty much the way he'd fallen through the door. My sweater is soaked from carrying him. I start to shiver in the cold room.

Val runs her hand under the body.

"His shirt is sopping. He's been lying out there in the rain since before it started to snow."

"Is that possible?"

"Oh yes. The human body is capable of amazing things when under great stress. Will it hurt if we look him over?"

"You're the closest thing we have to a coroner – it may be days before help arrives. Go to it. I'll take notes."

Expertly, from what I can see, she runs her hands up and down the body, bending limbs.

"Delbert went out to get more wood for the fire around four thirty or five. I remember him saying he heard Turk barking to be let in. I didn't see him after that. Also, the blow didn't kill him hypothermia did, but there is a big lump at the base of his skull." She studies the wound, which is plain to see.

"He was bleeding and exposed to the elements. My guess is he was unconscious – came to – crawled to the library door. Died as he fell."

She dries her hands on the felt of the billiard table. "Not a scientific conclusion, but it's the best I can do and leave things as they are for the police."

Val takes a hard look at me, "Hey, don't you collapse on me. I've got Herbert in the library. No telling what is happening upstairs."

"Cold, freezing. Feet like twin icebergs," as my teeth start to chatter.

"Get out of those wet clothes. The slushing sound I heard in the library was your shoes. You've got the beginning of a good-sized bruise on your forehead."

"Hit the steering wheel when I went off the road."

"Weren't you wearing a seat belt?"

"When that Jeep was made, they'd never heard of them."

"Have you had anything to eat? The closet in the hall by the front door has all kinds of emergency blankets and clothes – this is normal Maine weather. Take Herbert a blanket. I'll see what I can scare up in the kitchen and bring it to the library."

She pushes me out into the hall, locks the door to the billiard room – good idea, and disappears around a corner. I obey orders.

By the time I get back to the library, clad in dry duds some of which I'd found in the closet, the entire family is bombarding Herbert with questions and demands, while shouting at each other.

That's it. They don't talk to their cousins: they speak to a void, devouring each other like a praying mantis eats her mate once copulation is finished.

Not one word is said about the grim burden Valerie and I carried to the billiard room. If these are examples of my relatives from my father's side of the family, I'm grateful we've never met.

The woman who'd fainted is demanding her car be brought around as she isn't about to spend another moment in a house with a deranged killer running loose.

Val's clear voice cuts through the nonsense. "The front door is at the end of the hall, Aunt Hyacinth – you're welcome to use it."

"Valerie, don't be absurd. I'd get my feet wet and take a cold."

"Don't think so. Cousin Gilbert has been walking around all evening with wet feet."

The male of the bored couple speaks up. "Valerie, you're a good girl. You brought food. I could use a snack." He reaches for the cart Val pushes into the room.

"Then go to the kitchen and fix it. This is for Gilbert, who missed his dinner."

"Who is Gilbert? Never heard of him."

My girl, oops…better not think out loud, bent over the man, giving him a menacing grin that could kill a cobra at ten feet.

"Benjamin Simon Vest-Simmons, allow me to introduce you to your cousin, Gilbert Wayne Vest of New York City. The bottle blond is Milly, Benjamin's useless helpmate.

"Herbert isn't able to do introductions. The skinny one is Hyacinth Lawson. She is my aunt. She and my mother were sisters. I'm not sure how she ended up here unless she invited herself as there is no family connection."

The lady in question throws up her head in indignation while glaring at her niece.

"The man sitting next to her is Daniel V. Vest. He is Herbert's uncle and the family lawyer. You almost met Walter Toolens Vest. His mother, who thankfully hasn't come back downstairs, is Edith Amelia Toolens Vest. She and Herbert's mother were brother and sister who married cousins."

Her vivid mouth breaks into an impudent grin. "We're the rogues from the other side of the family. Your grandfather and my grandmother were fraternal twins, so I think that makes us second or third cousins. I'm Valerie Louise Vest."

"Thank you, Valerie. Gilbert will get everyone sorted out. Sit down and eat your dinner. Cold turkey sandwiches and hot cider spiked with brandy," Herbert adds.

"My favorites."

"Herbert, Mother could use a tray in her room and some extra firewood."

Valerie replies, "Which you will eat and use. Your mother was soused before she went upstairs. Walter, if you want a sandwich, try the kitchen. The woodpile is by the back door."

"I was speaking to Herbert. We're his guests."

"Yes, Walter, you are, but I didn't invite you. When Delbert died, the house became Cousin Gilbert's and mine. Technically, you're imposing on our hospitality. Now, go fix your sandwich and come back if you want. Herbert will tell the story once, then we'll all go to bed."

I don't say a word as Val is standing on my bare foot. To keep from yelping, I take another bite of an excellent turkey sandwich. I'm not sure which has produced a more profound silence – Delbert falling into the room or her pronouncement that we now own this damn house. One I sure as hell don't want.

His wife rounds on Benjamin. "I don't understand, Dear. Why does Valerie inherit and you are ignored?"

"Milly, I wasn't born when Grandfather Vest made his will."

"Herbert, do you want me to explain matters?"

"Please, Uncle Dan. It's crass to talk about wills and inheritances. My brother is dead. His body is lying forsaken in the billiard room. We don't know who murdered him or why."

The spiked punch is working for Herbert. His voice barely shakes. He appears calm, though his hands are gripping the arms of his chair, as if it's going to take flight.

146

Daniel Vest is about the age my father would have been if he'd lived. He has a mellow courtroom voice, designed to keep a cool demeanor in deliberations. People listen to him. He speaks low to command complete attention to what he has to say.

"It's rather mundane. My father explained it to me when I assumed his duties at the firm. When Grandfather made his will, Herbert was in the army, a dangerous place to be. He knew Delbert wasn't capable of managing his affairs, so he provided a means to cover the possibility of his grandson Herbert's premature death.

"He asked Delbert who were his favorite people. Delbert named William Gilbert Vest, Gilbert Wayne Vest's father and Louise Toolens Vest, Valerie's mother. They had grown up in this house.

"The old man then by-passed his son and willed the house to Delbert along with a trust fund sufficient to maintain the property. He named William and Louise as trustees, with the provision that they would inherit from Delbert. As the male Vests were serving in the military he appointed Louise Vest as administrator of the trust."

Walter interrupts him, "Mother told me she manages the family funds."

"Walter, in case you haven't noticed, your mother is a lush. She couldn't maintain anything long enough to use the Brooklyn Bridge to cross a mud puddle. She has a trust that is serviced by my firm, which you will inherit upon her death. Now please, let me finish, there isn't much more."

Valerie's aunt breaks into his explanation. "When Louise died, I should have been appointed to the trust."

"You are not a member of the Vest family, Mrs. Lawson. Besides, Valerie was of age when her mother died and agreed to assume her duties.

"As you know by the end of World War II, William G. Vest was the only male of his generation to survive and he was killed a few years later. All of his family inheritance passed to his son, Gilbert Wayne.

"Currently, Herbert Benjamin Vest inherits the bulk of the family funds from his father. Some years ago, he and Gilbert Wayne Vest made joint wills giving each other their assets to keep funds in the family. I suspect their reason is because neither of them has an heir.

"Herbert, I gather you neglected to inform Gilbert of Delbert's existence."

"Uncle Dan, Gilbert is the one who is always racing off to places like Bosnia where there are wars. Who would want to kill me?"

"Who'd want to kill Delbert?"

"You have a point, ugly though it is.

"Gilbert, I had no idea you didn't know about Delbert when your paper required you to make a will before going to Bosnia."

"Ben, does Uncle Dan mean you're out of the money?"

"Milly, my name is Daniel. I am not your uncle, but the answer to your question is yes."

Valerie leans over close to my ear and whispered, "Never discount Milly. She has a cash register for a brain."

Her brown eyes are dancing like a kid caught with sticky fingers by the jam jar. As each minute passes I'm finding Cousin Val is a gal who knows how to walk on mountains. I peek at my watch to make sure I've known her for a few hours because it feels like all of my life.

Milly plants her fists on her ample hips. "Valerie, are you talking about me?"

"Actually, I paid you a compliment. Your heart is in the right place."

Damn near get my fingers when taking a bite of the turkey sandwich to keep from laughing out loud. Daniel Vest swallows a slug of brandy for the same reason.

I clear my throat. "This inheritance business can wait till morning. Herbert needs to sleep off the spiked punch Valerie has been feeding him. Where is his bedroom in this mausoleum?"

Daniel answers. "Gilbert, I'll take him with me. Valerie, where is your cousin bunking?"

Valerie answers like she has been mistress of the establishment for a long time. "Herbert, put him in the blue room above this one. I'll show him."

"How is *our* monstrosity heated?" I ask.

Val hears my stress on the word 'our' and smiles. "Wipe the squint from between your eyes. Worry doesn't become you. Herbert has a lifetime vested interest before we have to take over. My telling Milly and Walter off got him laughing, not thinking of Delbert for a moment.

"The heating is oil, with an electric fan. An emergency generator powers the fan. It should last until the lines are repaired."

"Valerie, we'll take the cart back to the kitchen. Herbert wants to spend some time with Delbert before he goes up."

She takes the key to the billiard room from a pocket and hands it to Daniel Vest.

"Here's the key. Make sure you lock it when you leave. We didn't have any choice but to move the body. The police won't be happy about our meddling."

Herbert pats her on the shoulder before he stumbles to the door. "Valerie, thank you for your help. I'm rocking on my pins. Don't know what I'll do without Delbert. So much to do."

"Not a thing that won't be waiting in the morning. Daniel, help him."

Herbert is leaning against the doorframe as if his legs are about to give way. We quickly load the cart. Herbert holds the door as Daniel pushes it into the hall. They are followed by the rest of the family. Valerie comes over to stand beside me staring down into the dying fire.

"Is it always like this when Herbert throws a family gathering?" I ask.

"Pretty much. They're parasites who leech every penny they can from Herbert, always after him to put Delbert in an institution for the mentally retarded and sell this place. How did you get mixed up in a family like ours?"

"Luck of the draw. I could ask you the same question," I reply.

"Not tonight, but I am glad Herbert invited you. You look like you need to find a bed. That bruise is going to be a whopper."

"Don't care to wake up freezing. Let's see if I can bank this fire so it will hold through the night."

"Not a bad idea. Your Boy Scout skills will get a workout in the morning in the kitchen – must use the wood range for breakfast. I'll put out a casserole and biscuits so I don't have to cook."

Val helps me bank the fire. The others have already gone, as if they're accustomed to being waited on and don't need to think about trivial things like heat.

~ ~ ~

I find Val in the kitchen looking bleary eyed and haggard.

"Sorry, I didn't get much sleep. Turk kept barking most of the night."

"You believe that story Herbert told me last night?"

"What story?"

"About Turk being a ghost dog, who has been dead forty years."

"Don't be silly. Turk is Delbert's dog. He is a Border Collie, who looks strange. One eye is blue and one is brown. The breeder wanted to put him down, but Delbert had him fixed so the blood line wouldn't be ruined."

"Why would Herbert tell me that story?"

"To give the house a mystique. Old houses need a ghost to be respectable or to pull your leg – and to enjoy a laugh at your expense when you stumbled over him in the library. My mother told me the about the original Turk. He was Grandfather Vest's dog. Delbert named all of his dogs the same so he could remember the dog's name."

"Turk lead me through the storm to the house."

"Did he try to take you around back?"

"Don't know. As I was coming up the drive he disappeared."

She hands me a cup of much needed coffee. Black as sin – perfect. "I'm guessing, but I'd say Turk was trying to get help for Delbert."

"Makes sense. Did you haul in the wood this morning?"

"No. Mr. Hargraves walked up to get things started. He had the fire going in the range and had filled the tank to heat water when I came down. His wife, Ruby, will be in later after they've cleared a path. She's the cook, he helps keep the place and has for years. They knew your father as a boy."

A little plastic timer dings. Val opens the white enamel door to the old range. A blast of heat and the smell of fresh biscuits rush into the room.

"Help me get these pans out. We'll eat in peace here in the kitchen. The others won't be down till later, they keep city hours."

I take the multi-folded dishtowel she hands me and pull the glass casserole from the fiery furnace. She yanks out a pan of golden biscuits. We put them on the warm surface.

"Plates are in the warming oven." She points to a door by the stovepipe.

"Help yourself. I don't like cold food."

A jar of apple butter and a pot of whipped butter are on the table. We eat in silence with the coffee pot close at hand.

"I've made a pig of myself, but I can't remember a better breakfast."

"Ruby will be pleased. She made the biscuits and a casserole of eggs, potatoes, onions, peppers and cheese yesterday. She didn't know how many Herbert had invited for the weekend. All I did was stick them in the oven."

"It hit the spot. Now, what do we do?"

"I don't intend to run a short order service. I'm going to put the food in the warming oven and make another pot of coffee. Everyone can help themselves when they get up."

"I hope Herbert can sleep as long as possible. I don't envy what he has to face today. Do you mind if I look around outside?"

"Bring in some wood when you finish exploring – it's going to be a long day. Give me your plate and I'll wash up. After I finish, I'm going to sack out on the sofa in the library."

I cadge a pair of boots from the hall closet before I step out the front door to avoid any of the family who may have invaded the kitchen.

The rising sun casts glitters of rainbows across the frozen surface. The snow crackles under my feet as I slog my way around the house. I want to see the path Delbert must have crawled from the opposite direction.

The frozen snow is bloody against the library door. From the appearance of the gully he'd plowed, it didn't snow for long after he knocked open the library door. We were too busy to notice the weather, so I can't be sure but guessing, I'd say two inches fell during the night.

It's easy to work my way around to the back of the house to the haphazard chunks of wood beside a large stump. Carefully, I brush aside the fresh snow and get a surprise. Under the snow is a roller, like landscape people use to tamp down freshly laid sod.

"I taught Delbert to do that."

I almost jump out of the loose-fitting boots when the deep voice startles me. A large, older man wearing a plaid Mackinaw and a heavy trouper's cap is watching me.

"Taught him to do what?"

"Use the roller on the snow, instead of wasting time shoveling. In the early days, when the snows came, road crews used big logs with teams to open roads for travel. Stayed that way until spring."

"I assume you're Mr. Hargraves."

"Yes, brought the wife up to help Miss Valerie. We've a small place across the road from the gate. Came out to get the roller to tromp down our path."

A joyous barking explodes from the barn and races to Mr. Hargraves' side. Then the black and white Border Collie, with off colored eyes, takes a tight grip of my cords and pulls me toward the house.

"Turk knows you. That's his signal to follow."

"Saved my life last night when my rental Jeep took a leap into a ditch south of here."

"Wants fed more than likely. We're coming, boy. He wouldn't stay at our place last night."

"I'm Gilbert Vest."

"Know who you are. Miss Valerie, told us you arrived during the height of the storm."

Hargraves makes no comment about the frozen blood that covers the woodpile. It's obvious Delbert spent time working the path before he was struck from behind. The route I followed from the library door had been rolled under the fresh snow.

Dilbert must have been bending over to get an armload of split wood when he was hit. He fell over the freshly split wood. Whoever was responsible, finished the job by driving the double-bladed axe into his back.

~ ~ ~

Turk ducks behind the kitchen range after begging a biscuit from Mrs. Hargraves. Neither Herbert or Valerie is present.

To escape the Tower of Babel frenzy of demands for service my cousins are pitching in the kitchen, I close my ears to their voices. Walter Vest and Benjamin Vest-Summons sound as if they are trying to outdo each other for Mrs. Hargraves attention. She ignores both of them and fixes plates for her husband and Daniel, who enters the kitchen from the hall as I take off the storm boots.

I pour myself a cup of coffee and stuff a biscuit with one of the thick sausage patties Mrs. Hargraves has fried while I was outside, then retreat to the library. Turk follows me. I suspect the din hurts his ears.

The dog stops outside the billiard room and scratches the door. It opens wide enough for him to slip through. I can see Herbert's heavy signet ring on his hand. It's best if I leave them to their silent vigil of grief.

Valerie turns over as I come around the end of the sofa to put my impromptu sandwich and coffee on a side table. The fire needs stoking and more logs. When I finish and reach for my snack, her eyes open.

"Did you find anything?"

"What I expected. Delbert was hit by the wood splitting block. He lay there long enough to leave bloodstains on the pile, then he crawled. My guess – he was on his last legs when he reached the door."

"Did you get much sleep last night?"

"No, strange bed. But I didn't hear Turk like you did. I met him while I was out looking over the murder scene. He is in the billiard room with Herbert, mourning Delbert."

"They're the best company for each other. Save me a bite of that biscuit and I'll share this long sofa with you if you don't mind my feet in your nose."

I take her up on the offer as the sharp aroma of burning red cedar fills the room. The cold walk and heavy food knocks me out in minutes. I remember thinking, before I drift off, that despite everything that has happened, my journey home hasn't been bad when I end up sharing a lumpy sofa with a beautiful woman.

~ ~ ~

"Mother...Mother!" He is screaming at the top of his lungs.

"Walter, your mother isn't here."

"She's dead!"

"She what?"

"She's dead. There's…a knife sticking in…her chest."

I've never seen anyone move as fast as Valerie. She rolls to her feet and shoves them in her shoes, grabs Walter's arm, and pushes him toward the door.

My loafers are somewhat stiff from their soaking the night before, but I'm close behind.

We race up the steps, taking them two at a time. The door to Mrs. Toolens-Vest's room stands wide open but becomes crowded as Walter and Valerie try to enter at the same time. He yields to her. I follow them.

The room is a shambles, as if someone has made a hasty search of every drawer.

Walter's mother lies in the middle of the bed. A tray of food is dumped on the floor beside it. A large knife, I guess from the kitchen, is planted between her breasts. The sheets are blood-soaked. Valerie is bending over her, checking for vital signs with her right hand and pushing Walter out of the way with her left.

She closes the woman's eyes, which are staring at the ceiling. There's a look of mild surprise on her face. I can't be sure in the dim light, but faint bruises are around her lips as if her killer clamped his hand over her mouth to muffle the sound of her scream.

Valerie rises and faces us. "She's been dead since some time last night. Her skin is cold. Rigor mortis is beginning to occur. No, Walter. Don't touch her. We must leave her as she is. Lock the door and wait until the police can get here."

The officers are going to be busy when they do arrive, now that Herbert has two bodies for them. I don't volunteer to take any pictures, as I'm sure the police team is equipped to handle the situation. I only took the Polaroids last night because we had to move Delbert's body.

Seated on a long sofa facing the fireplace are the same four people. Now I know their names: Ben Vest-Simmons and his wife, Milly, Hyacinth Lawson, Valerie's aunt, and the family lawyer and Hebert's uncle, Daniel Vest. Their heads turn to face us as we enter the room. Same bored expression on their faces, almost like a time-lapse.

Four armchairs are near the fire. Walter heads straight to the chair closest to the heat that his mother occupied last night.

Herbert is in the opposite chair. He is staring into the blaze. His face shows the extent of his grief: he's aged ten years over night. Deep crevices frame his mouth as he, no doubt, ponders the senseless tragedy that has struck him. Delbert was not only his brother, but his twin brother. They had shared their entire lives together.

Yesterday, in the billiard room, Valerie had brushed back Delbert's hair to show me the ugly forceps scars. I couldn't help speculating if Herbert subconscious memory extended back to a time when they shared the same womb and his brother was normal.

Now, he motions for us to take the other two seats. Val takes the chair by Walter and reaches out to give his arm a squeeze. He isn't aware of her gesture of comfort and ignores her.

Herbert shakes his head then looks at me. "They have the phone lines repaired, got word a few minutes ago. Called the State Police, who handle big problems for the county. They estimate it will be three to four hours before the road is cleared. All we can do is wait."

"I want my car brought around as soon as they arrive. There's a maniac running around killing people."

"Aunt Hy, there are no servants in this house. You'll have to go out and get your own car."

"Delbert always brought it around to the front door when I've visited. Daniel can do it. I get a cold if I get my feet wet."

Herbert stiffens his spine to look at Hyacinth Lawson. "It wasn't Delbert. I would bring your car. I'd love to do it now because you don't belong here. I asked you not to come _ I told you when you arrived last week to go home."

"How can you say anything so untrue! You welcome me when I come to visit."

"We traded places when you visit and stayed for weeks. Besides, picking up after you puts too much on Valerie. I seldom get to see her or Gilbert. I wanted them to enjoy their visit."

"I'm going to my room to pack." She uses Daniel's knee as leverage, to rise from the sofa and starts to the door. He doesn't offer to help her.

"Aunt Hy, before you go. I suspect the police will hold everyone until they have completed their investigation."

"Don't be absurd. We were together, in this room when Delbert fell through that door." She points to the French doors as if they are the real cause of the murders.

My gal, Val, in a spirit of mischief adds more fuel to the fire. "You're forgetting Walter's mother."

"I most certainly am not. Poor woman."

"Where were you when she died?"

"In bed."

"Can you prove it? Was anyone with you?"

"Valerie, you're being vulgar. You started this obscene conversation."

"No, I'm trying to get you to understand those are questions the police will ask. Two people have been murdered. Each of us is a suspect. We're the only people present. Ghosts don't swing axes into a man's back or plunge knives into helpless old women who are sleeping off too much gin."

"Mother never took more than a small nightcap," Walter objects.

"We were in bed. Together," Milly pipes up.

"Yes, Milly. We know."

The room lapses into silence as we wait for the police. There is nothing to say. What can people discuss when their only connection is two murders. What did they know that I didn't? The stranger that I am knows nothing about this group of people other than by a nebulous quirk of fate, we are related by blood.

Valerie studies the fire. I watch her.

As if she can feel my eyes on her she looks up. "Gilbert, will you be going back to town?"

"My departure will have to wait until the Jeep I rented is out of the ditch. But I need to spend a few days in New York, before my vacation runs out."

"Could I bum a ride?"

"Certainly Val, I'd be pleased to have your company if you can trust that old wreck."

"I must get back to work. My supervisor wasn't too happy with my taking leave during the busy season.

"Herbert, I don't mean to walk out on you at this time, but duty calls, as I told you when you phoned with the invitation. There isn't anything I can do to make this easier for you."

"I know, my dear. You and Gilbert have jobs. Your staying here won't bring Delbert back. The Hargraves will help me. I was thinking of asking Ruby and Vernon to move up the hill and live here. It would be easier for them, as they aren't getting any younger."

"That's a brilliant idea. I won't have to worry about you being alone in this big house."

"Bless you. Valerie. You are so like your mother. You miss her, like I do Delbert."

Turk rises from beside Herbert's chair and crosses to the door, whining to be let out. Since, I'm nearest, I follow him. Instead of heading for the kitchen, he takes a nip of my pantleg and pulls me toward the front door. We reach it just as the knocker thumps.

Two State Police officers are on the threshold, and I for one am glad to see them. Turk is nervous about the strangers but gives way when I lay my hand on his head.

"You reported a murder to our office that happened during the storm?"

"I didn't, but my cousin, Herbert Vest made the call. The first victim was his twin brother, Delbert.

"Please, come in. Give me your coats. I'll hang them in the closet and take you to the library where you can speak with Mr. Vest."

"Wait a minute. You said 'first victim'?"

"Yes. This morning, Mrs. Edith Toolens-Vest's body was discovered by her son, Walter."

"I'm Detective Ramson Carter and this is my partner, Sergeant William Evans. Who are you?"

"Gilbert Vest, a cousin."

When I open the door to the library, Carter and Evans step back.

"Too many people. Could you ask Mr. Vest to speak to us, out here?"

I motion to Herbert. He reluctantly comes out and shuts the door behind him. I make the introductions and excuse myself, but Herbert stops me.

He tells them about Delbert falling into the library. His voice is firm and precise as if it's a story from times past with no relation to him. He didn't need my feeble moral support.

The officers are not pleased we'd moved the body, as we reasoned, but given the circumstances, it was a necessity.

He informs them I'm a reporter and had taken Polaroid photos before Delbert's body was moved. They want them and I fetch the photos from my carryall.

Herbert suggests I take Sergeant Evans upstairs to Mrs. Toolens-Vest's room, while he accompanies Detective Carter to Delbert's body. He hands me the key. It's a standard skeleton key which will open any room in the house.

The low fire has long since burned out and the room is freezing. Sergeant Evans walks to the bed, being careful not to disturb the debris. I go to a window to admire the view of the snow-covered fields glittering in the afternoon sun. I'm busy composing shots in my mind when I look down.

I have a clear view of the woodpile. "Sergeant, please come here."

"What do you see?"

"Look down. Delbert Vest was struck near that splitting block. I was out there this morning, before anyone was up and saw his blood stains in the snow. I followed where he crawled to the library door."

He studies me with shrewd blue-eyes. "Mr. Vest said you're a reporter. What were you doing, looking for a scoop for your paper?"

"Good heavens, no! My work is overseas. I arrived last night mere moments before Delbert Vest fell through the door."

"How often do you visit?"

"First time. You passed the Jeep I rented, about a mile or so below the gate in a ditch. I walked to the house."

"Some reception."

He goes back to the bed. I can't take my eyes off that woodpile.

"Has anything in this room been moved?"

"No. Valerie Vest, another guest, who is a nurse at Bellevue checked her body, then hustled the murdered woman's son, Walter out of the room and locked the door."

"Did she touch anything?"

"Checked for vital signs. Fingerprints? Mrs. Toolens-Vest's son's prints will be on the breakfast dishes. He dropped the tray when he found his mother."

"Our crew should be here by now. They will check for prints and take photographs before the body can be removed. Nothing more we can do up here until they're finished. Would you please join your family?"

As I start to the door, I take another look out the window.

Herbert and Detective Carter are walking toward the woodpile.

"That's it! That's why she was killed."

"What are you talking about?"

I point to the window. I'm excited, as I've managed to put together a plausible explanation for Walter's mother's death. "Sergeant, Mrs. Toolens-Vest liked her liquor. In the very brief time we were in the same room, she didn't say one word, just sat there, drinking with a very satisfied smile on her face.

"We discussed her death and wondered why an elderly woman was knifed in her sleep: she saw Delbert Vest's killer.

"A murderer can't afford to have an eye-witness. She may have confronted the killer or was seen standing in the window. Actually, no, people don't look up, which is why snipers hide in trees."

"Mr. Vest, 'snipers in trees?'"

"Sorry, thinking out loud. Occupational hazard, visualizing a scene before I shoot."

The Sergeant scratches his head and looks out the window. "The window would make a good stand if you were a hunter."

He misses my point. Walter's mother was dead and her killer is in the house.

~ ~ ~

The first thing I notice in the library is Valerie's absence. Even with the roaring fire, the room seems cold. Someone had overloaded the grate.

Herbert smiles. He must have noticed disappointment on my face. "Valerie is with Detective Carter, giving him her statement. I've already talked to him. As I've already told everyone, the detective insists on an interview with each of us."

"Herbert, it's ridiculous. We're being held here against our will. Delbert was your brother, but I barely knew Ethel."

"Hyacinth, I've tried to explain. If you have any more complaints, take them up with Detective Carter. I'm tired of listening to you."

"I most certainly will, rather than put up with your evasions. Daniel will express the family's concerns at this trying time."

Aggravated, Daniel retorts, "I will not. In a legal capacity, I represent Herbert, Walter, Benjamin, and to some extent Gilbert, and Valerie, who are all doing their best to help the officers. I do not represent you. Gilbert, did you learn anything upstairs?"

I don't want to evade Daniel Vest's question, but Walter is clearly not in any shape to endure a theory as to why his mother died.

"Not much, other than it will take some time for the police to finish their investigations before the bodies can be removed to the local morgue."

"Very well."

Valerie opens the door and holds it as Mrs. Hargraves pushes a loaded cart into the room. I'd lost all track of time until I sneak a peek at my watch. It's 2:30. My stomach must be off-kilter to ignore feeding time.

"Mrs. Hargraves, take that out of here immediately! Luncheon is served in the dining room."

"Aunt Hy, Detective Carter is working in there, where he can have some privacy," Val replies.

Val and Mrs. Hargraves clean off the big desk, covered it with a cloth and lay out a buffet. Patties loaded with onions, buns, plates of sliced tomatoes, lettuce, cheese slices, pickles, spreads, for build-your-own-hamburgers, baked beans, potato salad, chips, and a large bowl of mixed fruit, quickly appear. Two large pitchers of beer and a pot of coffee rounded out the spread.

"Thank you, Ruby. We often take our evening meal in this room by the fire."

"Mrs. Hargraves, I will take my repast in my room."
Hyacinth Lawson moves swiftly to the door.

Valerie stops her with soft-spoken words. "Aunt Hy, the upstairs is closed until the police have completed their investigation. Here is a plate, help yourself, then Milly and I can follow you. Mrs. Hargraves is not your servant."

Ruby Hargraves slips silently from the room without acknowledging her defender.

"You mean to tell me we're being held prisoners? Exiled from the solace of privacy in our own room? During this trying time!"

Valerie's laugh rings across the room, hardy and heart felt. "Stop behaving like a spoiled brat. There is enough to contend with, without you being a pretentious ass."

For an instant, a flash of hatred blazes in Hyacinth's eyes. It isn't directed at her niece, but at Herbert. She yanks the offered plate from Valerie's hand and turns her back on her.

Daniel Vest brings small tables near the sofa and chairs. We eat in blessed peace, except for a low, but earnest conversation between Herbert and Walter, out of our hearing.

~ ~ ~

Throughout the long afternoon, Sergeant Evans sticks his head in the door and calls one of the group to give their individual statement. I am last.

169

Carter fills out a form with the usual information, taken from my driver's license. He raises his eyebrows at my international license, checks the dates on my passport, and is kind enough to remind me it is due for renewal. "You don't stay in one place for long."

"No, I go where my editor sends me. Live out of a suitcase."

"This is your initial visit to your family home."

"Yes."

"Why did you drive that old Jeep all the way from New York?"

"Playing tourist. The weather was supposed to be nice. First vacation I've had time to take since my aunt died some years ago."

"One of my men brought it up. I'd advise you to turn it in at the nearest terminal and take a train or a plane back to New York. It's amazing the poor old thing made it as far as it did."

"Thank you. I'm not sure what you're free to tell me, but have you learned anything about the murders? To me, they appear random, with no purpose."

"That about sums up my conclusions. Hate to deal with these family things where there is no apparent motive, no clues, no particular relationships, no divergence in statements…a bland nothing."

A flash of the room I first entered, darts through my mind. An initial impression of blandness or lack of vitality, people existing, but not living.

Detective Carter gathers the stacks of forms and puts them in his briefcase. "We're finished. The bodies have been removed to the morgue. Mr. Herbert Vest will be notified when the autopsies are completed and the family may claim them for burial."

"Are we free to return to our jobs? Hospitals are always short on staff and Miss Vest has expressed concern."

"You and she are the only ones who don't live in the general area. I see no reason to detain either of you."

~ ~ ~

A strange peace settles over the house once the authorities clear the premises.

I'd ignored the jolt my back had taken when the Jeep took a nosedive, until I flex my shoulders and feel little stabs of pain shooting up my spine. I retreat to my room for a hot shower and a nap to relieve the delayed soreness.

It's after nine in the evening when, much to my own embarrassment, I wander down to the kitchen in search of nourishment. Valerie is sitting at the table, nursing a cup of coffee.

"I took a shower and died."

"There's a pot of clam chowder and fresh coffee. Everyone else is in the library. How are the muscles?"

"Sore. How did you know?"

"Gilbert, I'm a nurse. Get whatever else you want out of the refrigerator and join me. I'm going to have the fruit with ice cream and cake. Leftover patties are in the warming oven. Buns are in the bread tin."

We don't talk while we're eating. I can't think of anything to say that will hide what I'm thinking. How do you tell a woman you've known for twenty-four hours, you want to marry her?

"You wash and I'll dry."

We clean up the remains of our late meal and the used dishes in silence.

"It's time to face the music. I'm not sorry I told Aunt Hy off. I've been wanting to do it for years. She sees nothing but her own comfort. Mother avoided her whenever possible. She made me glad I never had siblings."

"I wouldn't know. I'm an only child myself."

Walking down the hall to the library she takes my hand and squeezes it. "We'll talk on the way back to New York. Now isn't the time."

"From what Detective Carter told me about the Jeep we'll never make it unless I rent a better vehicle."

"That idea has nice implications."

We're laughing as I hold the door for her. Walter, Daniel, Benjamin, and Milly are playing cards with martini glasses by their sides. Their manner says they've done the same, many evenings in the past.

Daniel greets us with a wave as he lays a small trump on the table, taking the hand.

"Herbert has gone out with Turk for a walk. Mrs. Lawson has retired to her room. Drinks are in the cabinet over by the door."

At my glance, Valerie replies, "I'll take a very light bourbon and water with plenty of ice."

While I'm fixing our drinks, I lean over and look out the glass door. "Want to join Herbert? It's a beautiful night."

"Yes, let's get our coats. The drinks will hold till we get back."

We hurry out the front door, to find a rare moonlit night. The air is crisp and still, not cold.

Herbert is walking down the drive, headed in our direction. Turk dashes to his side, holding a stick in his mouth. Herbert takes it and throws it as far into the field as he can. Turk darts away chasing the flying stick.

I glance toward the barn. A dark car without lights is rolling down the drive, picking up speed.

Valerie screams.

I run across the snow-covered lawn toward Herbert. A black streak flashes across the white field to reach his master.

The motor of the car roars drowns out my screams, gaining momentum as it heads directly toward Herbert.

My feet sink through the crust of the drifted snow, slowing my frantic effort to reach Herbert. I must pull him out of the path of the speeding car. It slides as the front wheels hit a patch of ice.

I grasp Herbert's arm, spinning him around so he sees the advancing car. Turk slams into him full force, throwing him into the bank of snow at the edge of the drive.

I feel the wind of the car before the back bumper hits my side, knocking me against a stone wall. I roll over fast as the front end of the car looms over me, scraping the wall inches from my face before righting and plunging down the drive at high speed.

I pull myself upright as the car slides, taking out one of the gate pillars, spins, rolls over and slams directly into a utility pole on the far side of the road.

The pole splits and topples across the car, sending giant sparks shooting into the night sky. The windows in the Hargraves' cottage and the house go black.

Herbert and Valerie are holding me up right. We watch in horror as the car literally melts under the high voltage lines.

"You took a hard blow – can you make it to the house with our help?"

"Yes." It's more a groan than a response.

I take one step and nearly pitch forward on my face. My entire left side is numb. "What about down there?"

"Nothing we can do until Vernon calls and complains about a downed power line. He has a short-wave radio for emergencies."

I know it's shock. I can't control it. Death is not new. I'd seen plenty of it, but never come so close to dying. My body starts jerking. My voice sounds high pitched and faraway.

"Who in the hell was the idiot driving that car?"

"Hyacinth Lawson."

"She tried to kill us!"

"Aunt Hy! Why?"

"Valerie, help me get him up to his room before he collapses. We'll talk later." Herbert's voice rings in my ear – cool, precise, and commanding. "Gilbert, you must hop on your right foot. Don't try to put your left down or you'll put us all in the snow."

I manage to obey, gritting my teeth to keep from screaming.

We make it to the front door. Daniel and Ben take over from Herbert and Valerie. They get me upstairs to my room where the world dissolves into nothingness.

As if in the distance, I hear Valerie talking.

"Two broken ribs, easy fix. Badly bruised. Help me hold this tape."

I awaken to find myself in bed, Walter sitting beside me reading a book.

He senses my movement. "Valerie is taking a nap. I'm nurse for the night shift. Do you need anything?

"Thirsty." Mouth feels like a coal train of dust has been dumped inside.

He reaches around my neck and shoulders holding my head up as if I'm a child. "Swallow these."

Four white pills are in his hand.

"What?"

"Aspirin. Only painkiller in the house. It helps if you chew them."

I swallow, their terrible taste lingering in the back of my throat.

He holds a glass of Coca-Cola to my mouth.

I try to push the sweet stuff away.

"Valerie said you were to drink it immediately after taking the aspirin. She said the heavy caffeine in Coke helped the aspirin to work faster.

"I wish I'd known that. Mother had terrible headaches in the morning."

~ ~ ~

Valerie keeps me prisoner in that room for three days. On the second day, I manage to walk around the room. The snow is almost melted except for piles along the drive.

Detective Curtis visits me for a statement, but I can add little to what he already knows. I tell him about watching Hyacinth Lawson drive her car, with every intent of killing Herbert Vest. He concludes the woman was criminally insane and we leave it at that.

Valerie tells me what happened as Herbert explained his theory concerning Delbert's death.

He believes Hyacinth killed the wrong brother first. As he told it, she had been trying to entice his mentally defective brother to marry her for years so she could gain control of the family funds, not fully understanding the careful provisions their grandfather had made for the twins.

Herbert had discovered her in the barn many years before making obscene sexual advances to his brother. I have no idea what Herbert attempted to describe in his Puritanical manner, but to me, the whole story was both repulsive and insane.

He agreed with me about Mrs. Toolens-Vest's death after checking the view from her window, making the sly comment that Aunt Edith wasn't above a spot of blackmail.

~ ~ ~

After breakfast on the morning we're to leave, before the others come downstairs, Herbert invites Valerie and me into the library for a private chat.

"Cousins, all families have secrets held by a spry elderly spinster who uses them to demand observance to their obsessions."

"But, Mrs. Lawson was neither spry, nor elderly, nor family for that matter," I object.

"No, she was evil. Delbert sensed it. He avoided her when she'd visit. I'm the keeper of the 'casket of secrets' for this motley collection of personages united by thin strands of blood."

Sensing the reference in his cryptic speech, I ask, "You mean 'casket of letters' as in Mary, Queen of Scots?"

"Child, that is what I enjoy about you. You don't let moss grown on your bones."

"Child? Herbert, we're the same age."

My spurt of temper pushes him into a sputter of indignation. "There is no casket per se, like she thought, which I suspect is why she searched Aunt Edith's room after she killed her. They are only memories hidden in my mind, by which I hold the family together. Family matters are not the business of the police."

"Delbert."

When Valerie says the name, Herbert jerks and looks directly at her, as he has not done since his brother fell through the door.

"It's time you told the truth," she replies, staring him straight in the eye.

"What do you mean?"

"The body in the morgue is Herbert's." Her voice is flat and challenging.

"How did you guess?"

"It isn't a guess. I knew the minute I examined the wound on the back of his head. Mother told me how to tell you apart. Herbert had a scar just above his left ear from when you pulled back a swing seat and it hit him, cutting a deep gash. It was stitched up with darning thread because this house is so far from medical help. The crude surgery left the scar."

She points to the dog lying in front of the fire with his head on my cousin's feet. "Turk. He's your dog and has hardly left your side since Herbert was killed. He saved your life and Gilbert's when Aunt Hy tried to run over you in the drive."

"Honestly, Valerie. We never knew who we were. Mama Har took care of us after our mother died."

"Who is Mama Har?"

"Vernon Hargraves' grandmother. She was half-blind and would mix us up when putting us back in our cribs. Vernon told me about what happened the day he replaced his father as our general handyman.

"We started trading places when we were little. Father wasn't here. Did we ever see him? I don't know. I have no memory of it. Grandfather Vest took care of our education. We never went to a regular school but had tutors. When he died that too stopped so we had little contact with the outside world until I was a grown man. Uncle Daniel took care of everything.

"After the news came that Father was killed in action, Grandfather didn't pay any attention to us. It wasn't until we were four or so and learning our letters that anyone noticed one of us was simple. Grandfather assumed it was Delbert because he was the last born."

"I see."

"Does it make a difference?" Despair clouds his voice.

"No, I don't suppose it does," Valerie said softly.

"Please, don't tell the others. It would cause Uncle Dan so many legal problems. After the formalities are observed Walter will move in here. He is near seventy and a lost soul without his mother. Aunt Edith squashed any relationship her cub might have formed before we were born.

"Benjamin can move in too, if he wants, after Milly dumps him. She will, now that she's learned he isn't going to inherit any of the Vest money.

"I don't see any reason why we should say anything about Herbert. It won't change anything.

"I miss Herbert. He wasn't a void. If I told him what to do and say, he did it perfectly."

"Yes. A twin is part of yourself."

We leave him gazing into the fire with his 'casket of secrets' dancing in his mind and go upstairs to pack.

When we come back down, I open the door to the library to say good-bye but change my mind.

Those who are left are sitting around the fire drinking martinis in a caricature of a 1930s movie.

Their single movement is to lift the glass to their lips.

# AUTHOR'S NOTES

Ever since Charles Eastman put cameras in the hands of ordinary people, strange images have been showing up on their photographs. On www.pinterest.com/nashblack05 we have a collection of photographs, carefully selected to the best of our ability, to show the presence of ghostly intrusions.

From time immemorial there have been stories told and accounts written of sightings and encounters with ghosts. Many of these have been passed off as delusions, myths, folklore, or tales told to children to frighten them. We are story tellers and our stories are solely for the purpose of entertainment.

But, what are ghosts? What is it, that creates a presence on otherwise normal snapshots? Is it a left-over energy field from a violent death conveyed as light to film since photography is product of recording light waves on film or a digital medium. Is phantasm that shows up on film "*a figment of the mind*" or "*a deceptive likeness*" as define in Webster's New World Dictionary, c. 2003.

For this collection of stories, after years of research, we've explored several aspects of the spirit world that have surfaced. With the advent of digital photography and a general public acceptance, the question of ghosts has undergone serious consideration, and, too much imperial evidence exists for the idea to be dismissed as mental delusions of misguided people.

Mythology of various cultures was once a common subject in public school's literature classes. Entire genres of modern fiction have been written, incorporating those stories into fantasy and paranormal fiction.

*Night washers* (an *ancient pagan belief*) occur as spirits at stream crossings, who washed the clothes of the dead at night. They dragged unwary travelers into the water to help them wash. If the traveler refused, or attempted to escape, they would break his arms and leave him to drown. Evil things they were, with hollow eyes that stared from empty sockets into one's soul.

Of the Grey People from the story, "The Shop" – were they ghosts or the extraterrestrials beings termed 'the Greys,' that emerged into our culture after the UFO crash at Roswell, New Mexico, in the 1940s? The story was written before we started watching *Ancient Aliens* on the History channel and learned of 'the Greys.'

In our research, we explored the Internet and are subscribers to Wikipedia, taking note especially of discrepancies and contradictions. For the phenomena of spontaneous human combustion, we found the section of Francis Hitching's *The World Atlas of Mysteries*, London, c. 1978, p. 20-23, the most comprehensive and enlightening.

# ACKNOWLEDGMENTS

We want to thank Barbara Jean Appleby. She is the author and illustrator of numerous titles of fiction for children, adults and non-fiction, plus coloring books that are sold on Amazon.com. She designed our logo for IF Publishing. We use her work to illustrate our online promotions, newspaper articles and blog. We know of no other person who can take a tiny idea with a poor description and produce the perfect illustration, often times the night before the article is due.

A big thank you to Charlene Perkins, who sold us the copyright to a photograph she had taken, for use as the cover.

There are not enough ways to thank our longtime friend, Paula Nason, for her time, patience, and diligent work in pulling our rough manuscripts together into a coherent whole. Her editing skills and insight into the stories and characters are invaluable.

Dean Fetzer, of GunBoss Books, www.gunboss.com, designs our publications, and brings them to the web, without his help we'd be lost in the world of independent publishing.

To the staffs of Kentucky libraries of Adair, Russell, and Pulaski counties, a heartfelt thank you for supporting us, both by adding our books to your collections and answering the many questions authors have when they research a story.

Jerry Sampson of *Sampson's Antiques and Books* in Harrodsburg, Kentucky, has carried our titles since the beginning. He gave us the thrill of a life-time when he devoted an entire window display to our titles.

Thank you to friends and family who understand when we disappear from the scene and forgive us for being out-of-touch.

# ABOUT THE AUTHORS

Nash Black is the couple of Ford Nashett and Irene Black, who combined their last names to use as a pen name. In 1988, Ford and Irene established *IF Publishing Company*, when they first began to developed their  writing careers and are working to master the fine art of social media marketing.

Their collected works have evolved into four distinct genres of crime fiction and paranormal activities: One County Series, Young Brothers Series, Capital Crimes Series, and Specter series.

They write for local newspapers and blog under the banner of Ono Almanac at http://onoalmanac.blogspot.com.

Irene and Ford can be reached through their website: www.nashblack.com.

Ford has a background in industrial x-ray work, mechanics, farming, retail merchandising, and auto racing.

For many years, he served as an observer for the United States Automobile Club.

Today, he follows racing at local dirt tracks.

He has been polishing his writing career since he wrote his first play in 1958. In his free time, he enjoys wood working, fishing, and photography. Ford can be found on Facebook, facebook.com/fnashett, and on Twitter @ovaltracker.

Irene has followed her passion for writing since 1954 when she saw her short essay printed in a national publication. Her love of books was exercised by over half a century working as a teacher and research librarian.

An accomplished naturalist, she has enjoyed a life-long interest in ecology, geology, and natural sciences. She is active on Twitter @pennhand and on facebook.com/irene.black.161.

They maintain their interest in the field of retailing with a small antiques business and in the graphic arts with two exhibits of their photographs each year, for the Fruit of the Lens Camera Club. which named their annual photography awards for them using their pen name, Nash Black.